THE BOOK OF BRISTOL

First published in Great Britain in 2023 by Comma Press.
www.commapress.co.uk

'Buckets of Blood' by Tessa Hadley first published in *Sunstroke and Other Stories* (Vintage, 2007). 'Going Down Brean' by Rebecca Watts first published in *Bristol Short Story Prize Anthology Volume 1* (Tangent Books, 2008). 'Public Performance' by Magnus Mills first published in *Screwtop Thompson* (Bloomsbury, 2010). 'A View From the Observatory' by Helen Dunmore first published in *Girl, Balancing* (Hutchinson, 2018).

A CIP catalogue record of this book is available from the British Library.

ISBN-10: 1912697637
ISBN-13: 978-1912697632

The publisher gratefully acknowledges the support of Arts Council England.

Supported using public funding by
ARTS COUNCIL
ENGLAND

Printed and bound in England by Clays Ltd, Elcograf S.p.A

MIX
Paper from
responsible sources
FSC® C018072

THE BOOK OF BRISTOL

EDITED BY

HEATHER MARKS & JOE MELIA

To the storytellers and story lovers
of Bristol's past, present, and future...

Contents

Introduction

IT IS IMPOSSIBLE TO capture the essence of a city, its multitudes, its contradictions, its extremes in a collection of just ten stories. As the writer, Aleksandar Hemon, puts it, 'there is no way to impose a self-sustaining narrative upon any city – only multiple, simultaneous plots/stories are possible.'[1]

Bristol is an old city. Its name comes from the old Saxon word 'Brycgstow', which means 'place at the bridge'. Situated on the River Avon and the River Frome in England's West Country, Bristol began with humble origins; it was recorded as a village in the Anglo-Saxon Chronicle of 1051, but archaeological discoveries in the area suggest there may have been human activity and settlement c.60,000 years ago. By the end of the mediaeval era, Bristol was a major port connecting Britain to France, Spain, Portugal, and Ireland, and was second only to London in terms of its maritime importance, earning its city status in 1542.

Bristol's competitive dance with London goes as far back as the 16th century. Sadly, this desire to emulate the capital would see Bristol surpass London two centuries later as Britain's premier slaving port. The transatlantic slave trade made Bristol – a city that was already wealthy – grossly rich, as Bristol ships, outfitted by Bristolian shipbuilders, stocked with Bristol-made cargo, sent out by Bristol merchants, transported hundreds of thousands of enslaved Africans from the West Coast of Africa to British colonies in the Caribbean. It's a history that can be seen in the city's architecture, its numerous estates, and, memorably, its statues: in 2020, at a Black Lives Matter march convened in response to the murder of George Floyd by US police officers, protestors tore down the statue of 17th century slave trader Edward Colston, that had stood in the city centre for two centuries, and dumped it in the River Frome.

While Bristol's past may have an ugly side due to its involvement in the slave trade, it also, as evidenced by the tearing down of Colston, has a radical side. Protest has long been a part of Bristol's constitution. In the late 18th and 19th century, the people rioted against new tolls (Bristol Bridge Riot, 1793) demanded better political representation (Queen Square Riot, 1831) and workers' rights (Black Friday, 1892). In the 20th century, the first anti-discrimination act in Britain came about as a result of the Bristol Bus Boycott (1963), which protested against the refusal to employ Black and Asian bus crews. Fast forward to the 21st century, and our city continues to speak up in support of human rights (Kill the Bill, 2021) and racial and climate justice.

Ask anyone to name something 'Bristolian' and chances are they'll say Clifton Suspension Bridge. The city is home to several feats of engineering by one of the most prolific figures in engineering history, Isambard Kingdom Brunel; his SS Great Britain, Great Western Railway station, and, of course, Clifton Suspension Bridge are instantly recognisable features of Bristol's visual character. Or they might say Bristol Beacon (formerly Colston Hall) and recall a gig they went to, or Aardman Studios - home to the makers of *Chicken Run* and *Shaun the Sheep* - or Balloon Fiesta, with a hundred hot air balloons rising off the ground at Ashton Court. Couple this with Bristol's buzzing food and music scene, street art, green spaces, and progressive politics, and you can see why it's often cited as one of the UK's trendiest places to live. But peer behind the iconic landmarks and famous graffiti and you'll see that in 2017, the Runnymede Trust and the Centre on the Dynamics of Ethnicity published a report that revealed Bristol to be the most ethnically segregated of the UK's core cities. Look further and you'll find that England's former second city has some of the wealthiest areas in the country adjacent to some of the most deprived,[2] with a stark divide in educational opportunities for young people in Bristol depending on where they live.[3] And yet, in the same year of the Runnymede report, *The Sunday Times* voted Bristol as the UK's best city to live, and Bristol is repeatedly voted as one of the best European cities to visit. So, how to approach a short story collection with a city of such multitudes as its subject?

There was a consensus among us, as co-editors, that we wanted to highlight stories which did not pander to the hot air balloon-filled vista of Bristol. That the stories in the collection feature areas and social strata of the city that present a wider picture of Bristol beyond its festivals, hen parties, stag do's, and raucous Fresher's Weeks. The stories in this collection stretch far and wide over the city, taking in the reaches of Hartcliffe, Withywood and Bedminster in Bristol's south; St Jude's, Easton and St Pauls to the east; and - in a dark twist on the leafy, affluent north - Clifton.

While Bristol may, as all cities do, have a tumultuous history, it also has a rich literary heritage. It was one of the first UK cities to have a public library provision, beginning in the early 17th century, though a library, of sorts, is said to have existed on Corn Street nearly 200 years earlier. The young poet Thomas Chatterton (1752-1770), who resided at the sexton of St Mary Redcliffe, was a precocious talent who influenced the Romantic greats, including Samuel Taylor Coleridge and William Wordsworth, before his untimely death at the age of seventeen. Coleridge and Wordsworth both spent significant time in Bristol and the first edition of their influential *Lyrical Ballads* was published by Joseph Cottle in 1798 in his bookshop on the corner of Corn Street and High Street; that publication set the style and atmosphere of much of Bristol's future literary production, namely its DIY and independent spirit. Other Romantic era connections include the poet and writer Ann Yearsley (1753-1806) who was one of few working-class women to gain literary acclaim at the time; the poet, playwright, philanthropist and abolitionist Hannah More (1745-1833), who initially patroned Yearsley and was an active campaigner for education of the poor; and Robert Southey (1774-1843), who was Poet Laureate of Britain from 1813 until his death.

Switching genres, academics and critics have posed that Mary Shelley, who visited Bristol in the mid 1810s, drew from the debates surrounding the slave trade as she developed *Frankestein*, that Gothic masterpiece and early example of science fiction. The poet and critic John Addington Symonds (1840-1893), who was born in Bristol and lived in the city for a large part of his life, was an early advocate of gay love and is widely credited with authoring the first literary study of homosexuality in the English language: *A Problem of Greek Ethics* (1873). Penguin Books, which revolutionised the publishing industry in the early twentieth century by making quality books available and affordable to a larger portion of the British population, was founded in 1935 by Bristol Grammar School pupil Sir Allen Lane. Angela Carter (1940-1992), best known for her magical realist short story collection *The Bloody Chamber* (1979), and widely acknowledged as one of the finest British writers of the post-war era, studied English Literature at the University of Bristol and set her first three novels in the city – *Shadow Dance, Several Perceptions*, and *Love* – collectively known as The Bristol Trilogy.

Bristol's current literary scene is as alive and vibrant as it ever has been. Bestselling and prize-winning authors of different stripes, including rom-com juggernaut Jill Mansell, historian and broadcaster David Olusoga (*Black and British: A Forgotten History*, 2016), YA author, screenwriter and memoirist Nikesh Shukla (*The Good Immigrant*, 2016), Costa Award winner, Nathan Filer (*The Shock of the Fall,* 2014), are based in the city, as are a plethora of exciting crime and thriller writers – C.L. Taylor, Jane Shemilt, Emily Koch, Gilly MacMillan, Charlotte Philby, and Sanjida Kay. Multi-award-winning science fiction writers, Cavan Scott and Gareth L. Powell, are part of a wealth of speculative fiction scribes in the city, with Stark Holborn, Virginia Bergin, Heather Child, MEG and Cheryl Morgan amongst many others who continue to develop a thriving scene.

Thousands descend upon the city for its literature festivals - including Bristol Ideas, Bristol Literature Festival, Lyra, BristolCon, Bristol Women's Literature Festival, Storytale, CrimeFest – which not only celebrate local talent but draw prolific authors from across the country and beyond.

There's a thriving publishing culture, with small but mighty independent presses such as Burning Eye Books, Tangent, No Bindings, Moot Press, Redcliffe Press, Sad Press, Bristol Radical History Group, Small Press Arkbound, Vika and Bristol University's hugely successful Policy Press. At the other end of the scale, the establishment of a regional office in the city by global publishing giant, Hachette, in 2021 is a signal of Bristol's continued and growing importance within the industry. This has been enhanced further with the birth of a new crime and thriller imprint, Baskerville, firmly rooted in Bristol and part of the Hachette stable.

There are a growing number of independent bookshops – Storysmith, Bookhaus, Max Minerva's, Gloucester Road Books, Arnolfini Bookshop, Forbidden Planet, Hydra, Heron

Books, The Good Bookshop, and the Small City Bookshop – to continue the legacy of those which have sadly closed their doors in the last few decades (including Chapter and Verse, Full Marks, Green Leaf, Clifton Bookshop, Wise Owl, and The Book Cupboard).

But it's perhaps in poetry where Bristol's literary scene is at its most dynamic, with a glut of poetry nights and events throughout the city such as Milk, Raise the Bar, BlahBlahBlah, Satellite of Love, That's What She Said, Tonic, Urban Word Collective, and Bristol Poetry Institute – that showcase wave after wave of big names and emerging talent to the spoken-word connoisseur, and build on the slam nights of the early 1990s. Malaika Kegode, Lucy English, Bridget Hart, Danny Pandolfi, Shaun Clarke, Vanessa Kisuule, Helen Sheppard and a host of others ensure the city pulsates with verse-filled energy.

So, what can one expect from the ten stories that comprise *The Book of Bristol*? Acclaimed crime writer Sanjida Kay's 'The Divide' is a psychologically taut story that takes the reader between wisteria-lined Clifton and the maligned St Jude's in a flaneur-like tale of the haves and have-nots. Artist and life writer Valda Jackson continues this magnified examination of stratification in Bristol in 'Team Players', a story set a year after the 1986 St Pauls riot, in which she subverts expectations of prejudice while acknowledging the insulating effects of segregation. Tessa Hadley's 'Buckets of Blood', set a decade earlier, is peopled with students from Bristol's other university; in a masterclass of deceptive simplicity, Hadley cracks the veneer of student life with a tale of a visiting sister. Nostalgia of a sunnier kind is to the fore in Rebecca Watts' charmfest 'Going Down Brean' which recounts a childhood trip to the west coast that many thousands of Bristolians will have made.

Menace, it seems, pervades much of the stories in this collection. In K.M. Elkes' 'Malago Days', a 'caff' (not cafe) in deep Bedminster offers respite, not just to the outside world but to the loneliness of old age. The late Helen Dunmore, a prolific writer who often wrote about lives in the margins of moments bigger than themselves, leaves the reader to assume the worst in a story overlooking Clifton Suspension Bridge. Rather than portray Bristol as a disturbing place, however, the stories weld the city's dark to its light so that one cannot be had without the other, and are often reversed in an instant. This mercurial quality is perhaps best captured in the poet Shagufta K. Iqbal's story 'The Cycle', a deeply moving tale of return and renewal that will resonate with anyone who's had to come back to their roots.

In keeping with Bristol's multifaceted nature, readers can expect to encounter many different genres within *The Book of Bristol*. As well as crime fiction, there are stories fantastical and speculative: Christopher Fielden's delightfully witchy 'The Baker's Zodiac' is a hilarious two-hander full of nausea-inducing spells and verbose demons, while 'The Water Bearer', by artist and poet Asmaa Jama, closes the distance between the coast of Somalia and Bristol's harbourside in a haunting tale of mermen and memory. And finally, in his trademark wry, sardonic style, Magnus Mills treats us to a memorable night at the Bristol Beacon as his young protagonist's new overcoat steals the show, in the author's respectful nod to Nikolai Gogol's 1842 classic.

While these stories cannot possibly do justice to the fullness of Bristol, they do, like a grubby little jewel, invite one to peer through the grime, view this city's different facets, and smile when it shines.

Heather Marks & Joe Melia
December, 2022

Notes

1. *Known and Strange Things*, Teju Cole.

2. *2019 English Indices of Deprivation within Bristol, compiled by The Ministry of Housing, Communities and Local Government.*

3. *2018 Bristol University School of Education research SOE 2018.*

The Divide

Sanjida Kay

THEY DIDN'T FIND HER until the dry spell when the water receded. Even then, it took a few days before anyone noticed. She had come to rest on a mud bank in the Frome, just outside the city centre. On one side of the river is a strip of grass, euphemistically called Riverside Park, which borders the M32; on the other, St Jude's, one of the most neglected areas of Bristol, home to the Salvation Army, a coffee roaster and a boxing gym, as well as, of course, the Pennywell Girls and two rival gangs. But the river had been sunk well below ground level and lined with high stone walls. Two boys had spotted her, when they'd dropped their BMXs on the verge and were balancing on the top. There were more sea gulls than usual and they threw cans at them. Until, that is, one of them saw her hand, half-submerged in the silt, and thought, at first, it was a mannequin's. But then he caught sight of her face. Emerald-green water weed had wrapped itself round her throat, which is why, to begin with, they also did not notice the necklace of dark maroon and livid yellow bruises.

★

It rattles and shifts inside the box as he turns it in his hands. He sets it back down on the table and wipes his hands on his trousers. He's left damp fingerprints on the maroon cardboard. He waves to the waiter and signals his empty glass. He's on his second Diet Coke already. It was a mistake coming here, to this posh restaurant near Queen Square; he'd wanted to make an impression, but the thought of eating a mussel makes him feel ill. He runs his finger round the edge of his collar. Everything is too tight and he can feel their stares: the other diners with their suit trousers, jackets slung over their shoulders; women wearing too much glitter. He'd told her to dress up. He'd thought to show her off. Get her out of those leggings and tunics she always wears, work that figure.

He checks his watch again. It's not like her to be late. She's the one who's always early, tapping one diamanté-encrusted nail against her Fitbit when he finally turns up. He talks too much to his clients, over-runs every time. It's why she suggested she have a key to his place so she didn't have to wait for him. And now, here he is, a year and a half after they first met, about to ask her to move in with him. He feels the waiter's eyes on him, like he knows he's been stood up. He stuffs the box into his pocket and swipes his card at the bar.

Maybe she's stuck in traffic – it's a long drive from Swindon to Bristol. She has a place there, only comes to stay with him one weekend a fortnight, and he thinks she'll say no – but it's time, time to move on, plan for a family. She's older than him, says she wants kids, and now, well, he's not exactly ready but he's getting there. He's just started a part-time degree in engineering, studying nights at City College, but after he's graduated and can get a decent job, he can provide for a family. Only so far you can go being a personal trainer at a council-run gym.

If his mum were still here, she'd say it was too soon, but he knows it isn't. *This woman saved me*, he wants to tell her. Wishes he could tell her.

'Alright Matthew?'

'Alright Sal,' he says, nodding to the woman standing at the corner of Wade Street in St Jude's, goose-pimpled in her too-short skirt and too-tight top.

He jogs up the stairwell of the apartment block on Pennywell Road; it stinks of piss and the lifts never work. His mum's flat, really, until she was deported. Fifty years since she'd lived in Jamaica, and they kicked her out. He knows that's what killed her: she had a heart attack as she stepped off the boat. They said it was hereditary angina, but he knows it was grief. Grief and shame.

No Dad. His mum said he was in the TA, training at the camp on Whiteladies Road. Disappeared back to Wales, or wherever he came from.

He checks his phone again. She hasn't replied to any of his texts. He tries to call her, but her mobile doesn't even ring. Like it's dead. The tightness in his chest makes it hard to breathe. He always worried about her coming to this neighbourhood on her own. His first thought, as he paces his sitting room, is to call the police. When it happened before, he'd gone home and watched TV. Sulked because she hadn't showed. He hadn't waited. He hadn't looked for her. He hadn't dialed 999.

But he can't. Not after last time. He stands at the window and looks out over the lights of the city. And he realises, as he leans his forehead against the glass and feels the chill of a February night on his face, that the flat smells strange.

It smells of bleach.

★

She had become entangled in a thicket of hemlock, almost three metres tall; their large, creamy-white umbrella-like blossoms had reached well above the height of the wall bordering the River Frome, whilst their roots remained in their watery bed. They ascertained that she had been killed before she was dumped in the river, but it was unclear where this had happened. When the city's most celebrated civil engineer, Isambard Kingdom Brunel, was alive, the Frome, which used to run like an artery through the heart of Bristol, was bisected and cauterised. The stretch where she was found is barely half a kilometre long. It disappears through culverts, winds beneath roads and pavements, emerges briefly by Ikea, slides through Eastville Park, and empties into the Floating Harbour where Brunel's beloved iron ship still sits.

What they could tell, though, was that she had been raped, both before and after she'd been murdered.

★

Every surface has been scoured; the floors gleam. He doesn't get it. She didn't come and meet him in a restaurant, but she's cleaned? He goes into his bedroom. The flat is nearly bare. He'd pawned most of the furniture after his mum had died: those bleak months before he met her. It seems even barer now. He doesn't know what's gone. He opens the drawers he'd cleared out for her: they're empty. He looks in the bathroom. Sometimes, when he misses her, and it's still a week until her next visit, he takes the top off her perfume, inhales her scent, rose and oud, and imagines he's kissing the soft skin behind her ear.

But it's gone.

Everything has gone.

★

4

The loneliness settles over him; like a coat at first, casually thrown on, and then he feels it sinking into his skin, embedding itself, welding with his tissue, his sinews. He passes the time with the girls on Wade Street; he talks to his clients; he speaks to the other students and his tutor on his course, but even when he's with them, keeping up the old banter, he feels alone.

Even though she'd only stayed two nights a fortnight, she'd kept the place alive. Sometimes she brought flowers from the petrol station on the M4; sometimes a bottle of cheap red from the corner shop, slipping Sal a fiver as she passed. Now it's dead; worse even than after his mother's death. He doesn't like to be there. He stays on at St Paul's Sports Academy in between clients, slouched on the metal chairs by the window, looking out over the M32 as he reads engineering textbooks; stays late at the library on College Green after his lectures.

It's like she didn't even exist. There are only his memories and the thought of her scent. No trace except for the bracelet he bought in St Nick's market when he was going to ask her to move in: silver with turquoise stones. He doesn't even know if she'd have liked it.

If she'd have said yes.

★

'She's left you, mate. Face it.'

He's old, in his forties, belly softening over his belt. Paul Weston.

The other officer is Violet James. The name doesn't seem to suit her: she's thickset, well-built, kind. Violet gives him a sympathetic look. She's blonde, hair tied back in a messy bun, purple smudges under her eyes.

He shakes his head, leans over his knees. He knew the police wouldn't take him seriously but he doesn't know what else to do, where to go.

He loved her. She loved him. He thinks of her beneath him on the new Ikea mattress she'd bought them: laughing up at him. No one had kissed him like that before.

'It doesn't make sense,' he mutters.

He thinks of the flat, the bleach. Had something happened there? They can still detect blood even if it's been wiped clean: he's seen it on TV. Nothing can get rid of blood.

'There's not much we can do. She's an adult. Free to come and go as she pleases,' Paul says. 'She got no friends? No one else has reported her missing.'

'There's no evidence of foul play,' Violet says gently.

'Her Facebook page has gone,' he says.

He'd wanted to see the selfie they'd taken when they went to the new gelateria in Easton, eating a giant peanut-butter, choc-chip and cherry sundae, both leaning in at the same time, grinning, whipped cream on their noses.

She was so pretty: black hair, blue eyes, the skin by her hipbone so pale, like she'd never sunbathed in her life. She'd picked him: she'd seen him in the pub on St Marks Road and come over. He wouldn't have dared talk to a woman who looked like her. And then she'd booked a personal training session with him. Halfway through, when he was trying to get her to do mountain climbers and push-ups, she'd stood up and smiled. Told him she'd only come to ask him out and she didn't give a fuck about interval training; said she was going now, and here was her phone number.

Paul yawns.

'I'll get us a coffee,' he says to Violet.

'And you don't have an address for her in Swindon?'

He shakes his head. He'd never needed it.

'Place of work?'

She'd worked for a finance company, drove out to clients round the south-west giving them advice. Boring, but she'd liked meeting people, she'd told him. Once he'd peered into her car – the parcel shelf had been missing, and he'd seen steel-toe capped boots, a high-vis jacket and a helmet. When he'd asked her, she said she'd borrowed them. Had to visit a building company and meet the guys on site, in a Portacabin with instant coffee in mugs that dirty she hadn't wanted to touch them.

'So glamorous,' she'd said, and rolled her eyes and laughed and kissed him full on the mouth, like she was melting into him.

How could she have gone?

He runs the tiny figurine of St Jude up and down on the chain around his neck. His mum's. She'd given it to him before she'd been chucked out.

'She's not listed as an employee,' Violet says. 'Maybe she was a consultant?'

He nods and shrugs and she says, 'Let me check the electoral roll. Give me her full name again.'

'Eden Adams.'

Saying it like that, sitting inside the refurbished police station on Trinity Road, the carpets still with that new-carpet smell, it sounds like a made-up name. Like a kid playing dress-up.

Violet shakes her head.

'Nothing,' she says, and she looks at him as if she's not quite sure what he is.

★

It's June, mid-morning on a Sunday, and he leaves St Jude's and heads to Clifton. His tutor has given them an essay to write on Isambard Kingdom Brunel, tells them to go and see what the man created for themselves. It would be three bus rides, so he walks – along the river, through the docks, ducking beneath the SS Great Britain. He can't afford the tour, but he picks up a leaflet from the ticket desk which tells him that when she was first launched in 1843, she was the largest ship ever built. He never came south of the river, or even to the north of the city, with her. Eden said she preferred the buzz of Easton and St Paul's. He crosses the Portway, and with Leigh Woods at his back, he climbs The Zig Zag, a steep, winding path cut into the cliff.

Near the top, he turns and looks across at the Suspension Bridge, slung, like an engineer's dream, across the chasm of the Avon Gorge. The bridge is suspended from cables between twin towers – from his reading he knows it spans a distance of 214 metres, weighs 1,500 tons, and was begun in 1831. Impressive, he thinks. Built for horses and carts and now carries four million cars a year.

Below him the tide is out and the mud glistens. It reminds him of Chelsea. After it happened, he couldn't look at her face, only her hands; river silt embedded under her raw fingernails. She'd been tough. She'd fought them. He'd wanted to wash the dirt and the dried blood away. But he wasn't allowed to touch her.

Although he's warm from the slog up the hill, there's a cool breeze from the river. He turns in the other direction, towards Clifton, its beautiful houses rising straight from the rock face. It's a part of the city he's never visited. He knows it's where those with money live. There's a pub with a garden set into the cliff, overhanging the Avon. It's crowded with people; the smell of roasting meat drifts towards him. A flash of crimson catches his eye. It's a young woman in a red dress; her arms are bare and her hair is black. She throws her head back and laughs. He can't hear her from this distance, and it's as if he's watching a silent film. He'd recognise the way she laughed anywhere. Is it her? She looks different, but he's too far away, he can't tell.

He sets off at a jog, a last slog up the slope, and down Sion

Hill to the pub. From street level it seems smaller, diminished somehow. He walks inside, pushes through the throng to the terrace at the back. The river is directly below him, a thin pewter line slipping between the mud banks to the docks and the sea, and he has a perfect view of the bridge. Isambard Kingdom Brunel, who died before it was completed, called it, 'My first child, my darling...'

He gradually realises that everyone here is white: students with thick, dark-blonde hair, older men in salmon-pink chinos, women in white jeans that cost more than he earns in a month. He's wearing his black Bristol Boxing tracksuit and they look at him like he's going to steal the silver or offer them a joint.

She isn't here.

★

It plays over and over in his mind – the woman in the red dress, throwing her head back, her throat a fine white line. Did he imagine that moment? Has he been looking so hard for her that all he can see is her echoed in other women?

He keeps returning to Clifton. After he's finished college, he heads straight up Jacob Wells Road and winds through the narrow streets, and by the time he's reached the top, the sky has darkened to a thick band of lavender over Leigh Woods and the lights of the city shimmer beneath him.

He finds places he's never seen before: curved honey-coloured terraces with iron balconies, mansions draped with Virginia creeper and wisteria, a theatre, locked communal gardens, Clifton College, The Engineer's House; the quiet is unnerving, broken only by the plaintive wail of lemurs trapped in the zoo.

One day in autumn, someone pounds on his door. When he opens it, it's them: PO Paul Weston and Violet James.

He looks at Violet and sees the softness in her face has hardened.

They've found out.

He lets them in and they stand in the middle of his almost-empty sitting room. He tries not to think about the day Eden danced across the floor in her bare feet, singing the blues.

'You didn't tell us you had a prior,' Paul says.

He says nothing.

'Previous girlfriend also went missing. Chelsea Phillips. Two years ago. Sexually assaulted, strangled and dumped in the Frome.'

He crosses his arms. Here we go.

'You know that, then you know it wasn't me.'

'Your mum gave you an alibi. Mums are good like that, aren't they?'

'If I had anything to do with that, or with this, do you think I'd have come to you? Told you Eden was missing?'

'You tell me,' says Paul.

There's a triumphant gleam in his eye.

'Very convenient there's no trace of Eden Adams. Was that her real name?' says Violet.

'And where is your mother anyway?'

He presses the figure of St Jude against his chest, runs it up and down the chain as he listens to them. Even though he knows there is no evidence against him, he feels his ribs tighten, because who needs evidence when you have a young black man with a murdered girlfriend, who claims another white woman is missing, and the one person who vouched for him is in a graveyard he's never visited, in a country he's never been to?

'You've been spotted,' Violet says. 'Lurking about in Clifton. Residents have reported you, and we picked you up on CCTV.'

'Looking for another victim, were you?'

They question him for two hours. He manages to remain outwardly calm; after all, he's been through this before. Last time he took up boxing so he'd punch the bag and not them.

'Stay away from Clifton,' Violet says.

'We're watching you,' Paul says, poking one finger in his chest as they leave.

He wipes the sweat from his palms on his jeans.

Two years ago, the coroner had concluded it was drug-related violence even though Chelsea had never done anything more dodgy than a Jägermeister in her brief life. He knows he was lucky; that being black and her boyfriend could have been enough to convict him then, and might well be in the future.

They're waiting for another body to turn up in the Frome.

Another young woman that someone has savaged. And this time, he's got no one to tell them where he was.

★

On Christmas Eve he calls PO Violet James. He doesn't know who else to turn to and the whisper inside his head is drowning everything else out.

'I remembered the registration of her car,' he says, thinking of the mud-encrusted steel-toe capped boots, the coil of rope on the backseat of her Fiat.

'Not going to help,' she says. He can hear her fingernails tapping on the keyboard. 'It was scrapped by a breaker in Avonmouth.'

He feels the tightness in his chest loosen. At least it's a sign that she existed. Maybe they'll listen to him now.

Violet takes a small breath. 'Right around the time you said your girlfriend went missing.'

'Who owned it?'

'Not Eden Adams,' she says. 'The car was registered to a company - IKB Engineering.'

He looks it up. The firm has a logo like a simplified version of the Clifton Suspension Bridge and an office in Kemble, another in Chippenham. He checks with Companies House and finds it's registered to a house in Clifton.

That evening he walks there. He goes the long way round, past the docks and along the Portway; the trees across the river are stark, lime-green with algae. He climbs up Bridge Valley Road, through a beech-lined avenue and emerges by an Observatory that was once a windmill. He can smell decaying leaves and his breath coalesces around him.

He knows it's the right house when he reaches it. There's a discrete chrome plaque on the sandstone gate post with an etched logo of the Suspension Bridge. It reads *IKB Engineering*, and in a smaller font: *Isabella Khalil-Brown*. There's a string of letters after her name.

It's a grand Georgian house, a basement with a kitchen, three floors, and what were the servant's quarters set into the eaves. He pulls his hoodie up, steps into the shadows, steps closer. Light blazes from the windows. The rooms are huge, the ceilings high: his entire flat would fit into the sitting room. There's a fir tree that's nearly three metres tall. It's real, and is decorated entirely with white baubles and wooden snowflakes. He hasn't even taken out his mum's old one this year: plastic, the tinsel balding, the lights missing bulbs, everything multi-coloured. There are giant shale-grey sofas and hundreds of cards strung from scarlet ribbon in front of an enormous fireplace. The fire is real too.

She's there. Eden Adams, or rather Isabella Khalil-Brown, in a red velvet dress, sipping a glass of champagne. She looks different: it's the way her dress flows, the light slides down her hair, the diamond on her finger glitters, her nude nail varnish gleams.

She must have worked so very hard to look cheap.

He can feel his heart hammering in his chest and his breath is shallow.

An older man, dark hair greying at the temples, leans over and kisses her cheek, pours himself a glass of champagne. He's Asian, skin the colour of milky tea. Maybe mixed-race. Probably her husband.

A year and a half, he thinks. *A year and a half of living a lie.*

It's as if he's been punched through the solar plexus with an engineer's scriber.

The anger rises up inside him then. He's suppressed it for so long, for more than two years: that quick succession of death and injustice, to his mum, to Chelsea. He strides down the drive, still sheltered from sight by the boughs of a magnolia.

He'll tell him, he thinks, he'll tell her husband what that bitch has done.

Two more people enter the living room. The resemblance to Isabella is striking – the older woman has her bright blue eyes and thick hair; the man's profile is identical. Her mother and father. They're beaming. The father is holding something out. All four of them crowd around, their faces lit up as if the small bundle is on fire. Isabella takes it from him and holds it up, throws her head back and laughs, her throat a long, white line. She slides the baby onto her hip: a little girl in a white and silver dress, a shock of black hair, big brown eyes.

For a moment he can't breathe.

It's his.

She has stolen the life he thought he had. She has stolen this baby from him.

He stops at the bottom of the stone steps leading to their front door, his hand gripping the iron railing, the metal so cold it sears his skin; his heart still pounding. He looks up at the house towering over him. Below him, the whole of Bristol is laid out, lit up like a Christmas tree; in the distance, the first stars of the night are suspended over the silhouetted hills of Somerset.

All this will belong to his daughter.

His hand goes to his throat, and he touches the necklace, rubs it between his fingertips.

Jude the Apostle, his mum had said when she gave it him, *patron saint of desperate cases and hopeless causes.*

He hangs it on the door handle, steps back into the shadows, and walks away.

Baker's Zodiac

Christopher Fielden

I

FROM THE HIGH BRANCH of a Bristol whitebeam, Hilda watched the bull. It was wandering around the herd of Devon Reds in Leigh Woods, sticking its whatsit into anything too slow to move out of its way. The bull cornered and mounted another heifer. The cow ignored him and chewed on a cud of luscious grass, waiting patiently for the ordeal to end. *Just like my Harold and I*, thought Hilda, *before he* –

'How we going to get it, Hild?'

'What?' Hilda snapped. Mildred had an annoying habit of interrupting her thoughts when they turned to Harold. Or, more accurately, whenever they turned to anything that wasn't Mildred.

'It's bloody huge and we ain't got no opposable thumbs.'

'What *are* you talking about, Mildred?'

'I've possessed a crow and you've…' Mildred glared at her. 'I'm not sure what you've possessed, but between us, we don't have no hands.'

'A pine marten.'

'What?'

'I've possessed a pine marten. It's of the weasel family in the order Carnivora.'

'Looks cute. Don't matter none though. I got wings and you got claws. How we going to milk it?'

Mildred raised a valid concern, but Hilda was in no mood to admit it. 'Milk it? Milking is what you do to cows, Mildred. Bulls are different.'

'What do you call it then?'

'I don't know. But not milking.'

'Call it what you want, that bloody thing is so randy there ain't going to be any...'

'Discharge?' Hilda suggested.

'Yeah... discharge. There won't be none left.'

Spells. Everyone seemed to think that magic was there to be used willy-nilly; that spells were easy to cast. Subtle tricks – lights, noises, moving something small from here to there – were easy, if you happened to be standing near some ley lines and practised regularly. Complex hexes that did something useful were different. If Hilda had learnt one thing over the past seven decades, it was that you *really* had to want to cast one to bother trying.

The hex Hilda and Mildred planned to cast was from *Mistress Birdwhistle's Cauldron Cookbook*, a tome filled with intricate incantations. Each required multiple ingredients, most of which were hard to obtain, some almost impossible. They were currently attempting to gather the final ingredient, which had to be fresh, potent and collected using the body of a possessed animal.

'So, how we going to get it, Hild?'

'Shush, Mildred. Let me think.'

'You'd better think quick. Night's comin'. We ain't got long.'

Hilda was tired. Every spell she cast these days made her feel closer to the Ever, but on this occasion, a step towards death would be worth it. It *had* to be done. For Emily.

She looked at the orange sky as it lit the rocky sides of Avon Gorge. Small, dark clouds glowed against a sun that was already kissing the horizon. *Focus. Do what you came here to do.* Hilda closed her eyes and cleared her mind. The answer was obvious.

'I have an idea, Mildred, but you're unlikely to approve.'

'Try me.'

'I'm going to possess-hop to one of those cows,' said Hilda.

'Ooo, that's good thinking. Like it so far. Which cow?'

'Does it matter?'

'Pick one he'll find attractive. A sexy one. With massive udders.'

Hilda looked at Mildred distastefully. 'I don't think he's all that fussy, Mildred. Besides, you know that possess-hopping can be random.'

'True, Hild, true. Just an idea.'

'I'll let him do his thing,' Hilda continued. 'Then we'll get... you know... what we need.'

'Discharge.'

'Yes, that.'

Mildred cocked her head and observed Hilda with a beady black eye. 'Get it how? We can't take stuff back what's inside creatures we possess, can we?'

Hilda shuddered. That would make an awful mess.

'Only what's on 'em,' Mildred continued. 'So if it's in a cow, how we going to collect it? This is the bit I ain't going to like, eh?'

'I was thinking we should employ a new and untested collection method.'

'What's that then?'

'Crow sponge.'

Hilda sensed that if Mildred had been in her own body, her hands would now be welded to her hips. In crow form, her wings flapped.

'Oh no, I ain't being no receptacle for bull seepage, Hilda Jane Beauchamp. I got standards. Besides, feathers ain't known for their sponge-like qualities. Fur is.'

Blast, thought Hilda, *she's always right.* 'Fine, you possess a cow. I'll…' her nose wrinkled, '…absorb the ingredient.' Hilda thought she discerned a glint of satisfaction in the crow's eye. 'Just get on with it, Mildred.'

'OK, I'm off. See you back home.'

II

Hilda woke in her armchair.

'You alright, Hild?' Mildred was squeezing her hand. 'You been out for nearly an hour.'

'Yes, yes. Baths always leave me drowsy, you know that.' So did witchcraft – her naps were getting longer each day.

'And you really needed a soak, Hild. That discharge made a right mess of your hair. You shoulda seen it. Like a punk's, it was. Sticking up all over the place – '

'I'm making a rule,' Hilda snapped. 'We will never mention this event again. Understood?'

'Alright, Mrs Grumpy,' said Mildred. 'You look like you need a cuppa. I'll pop the kettle on.'

'Have you checked on Emily?'

'Not for a while.'

'Every half hour, Mildred. That's what we agreed.'

'I been trying to get the cauldron ready while you been snoozing. I can't do everything, Hild. Some help'd be nice.'

Hilda held her hands up. 'I'm sorry. I'll look in on her while the tea's brewing.'

As Mildred stomped off into the kitchen, Hilda pushed herself out of the chair. Her back clicked, her knee popped. Even napping was tiring, which defeated the purpose. She tutted. Ageing was annoying her more than Mildred.

The cottage's stone stairs were steep and awkward, but Hilda refused to install a stairlift. That would be admitting defeat. No, she'd be resting eternally before Stannah were permitted anywhere near the house. She peered from the circular window on the halfway landing and saw a waxing, gibbous moon in a star-filled sky. Bristol's lights twinkled beneath. Fireworks erupted across Withywood and Bishopsworth. From their location on Dundry Hill, the witches would often watch people celebrating on the 5th of November. Hilda had planned to enjoy the view with Emily this year while Janice worked a nightshift – to share quality time with her granddaughter – but it was not to be. When Emily had pulled the Ouija board from her backpack with a hopeful look, Hilda should have said no. The magical location of their home was a dangerous place to engage in such a game, but Hilda had thought herself experienced enough to keep Emily safe while she nurtured her granddaughter's interest in witchcraft. In hindsight, the decision provided further evidence that age was taking its toll on her, both mentally and physically.

Hilda hauled herself to the top of the stairs and approached the third bedroom. She listened at the door. All was quiet. The door creaked open with a gentle push.

Emily was floating above the bed, bathed in moonlight. The small girl was wearing pyjamas and clutching a cuddle-worn teddy bear. Hilda had expected this. Levitation was a normal side-effect when the subject was contained within a stasis spell; as the possessing demon fought the magic bonds, energy would build and, as it discharged, weightlessness could occur. What Hilda had not expected was Emily's face…

Nothing was where it should be. Her nose was upside down, located where her left ear should be. Her mouth and jaw were sideways so they appeared vertically on the right side of her head. One eye was in the middle of her face while the other was in the V of her top lip. Both eyes shone with alien phosphorescence. An ear had replaced her chin. Hilda couldn't see the other one. Emily's curly blonde hair was the only thing that was almost in the right place, but it was sitting lopsided, as if the crown of her head was too far back and to the left.

Tears welled in Hilda's eyes. *What have I done?*

Mildred arrived behind her with two teacups on a tray, accompanied by a plate laden with bourbons.

'Oh Hild, don't cry. We can beat it. Have a choccy biccy.'

Hilda took a biscuit, nibbled it for comfort, and then said, 'Look at her poor little face.'

'Ooo, blimey, we can't give her back looking like that. Your Janice'll throw a wobbler.'

Janice would throw more than a wobbler. She didn't understand or approve of witchcraft. How could she? The gift always skipped a generation and Emily had not made things easy. She was stubborn — a relentless question asker.

Hilda knew that discouraging Emily's interest in the occult was folly. When she'd first perceived her own gift, Hilda had found it irresistible. There was no choice — to oppose it would have been as futile as refusing to eat. She had decided to encourage Emily, to help her explore her gift safely...

Silly old fool. Witching was dangerous.

This is all my fault.

'Staring ain't gonna fix it, Hild. It's almost eleven. Best we get started on this banishment hex. Come on, we's powerful witches.'

The conviction in Mildred's voice allowed Hilda's composure to return. She twisted her wrist and dislodged the whitebeam-wand concealed up her sleeve. She waved it gracefully and muttered a few words to maintain the stasis spell's hold. Mist, filled with miniscule sparks, seeped from the wand's tip and swirled around Emily, gently guiding her back down to the bed.

'Let's get to work.'

III

The cauldron was positioned in the hearth of the cottage's kitchen, above the embers of a large fire. The location of their home allowed access to St Michael's ley line, which ran from Land's End to Hopton-on-Sea on the Norfolk coast. Hilda drew on the ley line's aura as she sprinkled a cup of Saharan sand into the cauldron, performed a single buffalo step, and muttered an incantation. A small whirlpool appeared in the centre of the pot and the broth began to fizz.

'Quick, Mildred, maintain balance.'

Mildred pirouetted around the kitchen, recited a charm, then dropped two icefish into the eddy. As the viscous liquid calmed, the witches leant forward and savoured the bouquet. The key to successful spell casting was equilibrium. Sand of the desert, tempered by fish from the –

A burst of fire erupted from the middle of the cauldron and the witches lurched back.

'Has that taken me eyebrows off, Hild?'

Hilda looked at Mildred's blackened face.

'No, but you do need a bath.'

'I ain't getting into it after what you scrubbed off in there.'

The contents of the cauldron bubbled with growing ferocity.

'The balance ain't right, Hild.'

'Stay calm, Mildred. We've used ingredients represented by all twelve zodiac signs, correct?'

Mildred checked the list. 'Saharan sand for Scorpio, them rare fishes for Pisces. That… you know… bull goop for Taurus. Yeah, I think we done good.'

The cauldron was boiling now. Mini geysers spurted scolding jets of purple steam into the air.

'We must be missing something,' said Hilda. 'Let me see the recipe.'

Mildred handed over *Mistress Birdwhistle's Cauldron Cookbook*. Mistress Birdwhistle had trained Hilda in witchcraft. Her teaching style was memorable – she didn't give answers, instead she deliberately held back information. It made her students think; there was always something cryptic in every recipe or spell she devised – something missing, so that those who lacked occult training would not be able to use them. The book was open at 'Baker's Zodiac: a hex of demonic banishment'. The twelve ingredients they'd gathered and utilised were adequate. Hilda skimmed the directions and looked for some cryptic clue… and smiled.

'What you grinnin' about?' asked Mildred.

'It's so obvious. It's in there twice.'

'Ey?' Mildred peered over Hilda's shoulder. 'Hmmm, I ain't had a nap like you.' She held up what was left of a melted ladle to emphasise her point. 'Care to share your wisdom?'

'Once the potion has thickened, we *bake* it. The spell is called *Baker's* Zodiac.'

Mildred caught up quickly.

'A baker's dozen is thirteen, Hild.'

Hilda smiled at her sister. 'That's right, Mildred. We're missing an ingredient.'

'But there ain't a thirteenth sign of the zodiac.'

Droplets of liquid spat from the cauldron and fizzed on the floor like acid.

Hilda thought quickly.

'Buns.'

'I beg your pardon?'

'Bread. Cake. The thirteenth ingredient should be something made by a baker.'

'Oh, you know what I got yesterday? Some Clarks Pies.'

'Perfect. Where are they?'

Mildred opened the larder door, rummaged around, and

returned with two delicious looking pies and a look of disappointment.

'They're scrumptious you know, these pies. 'Specially with some chips from The Magnet. Bit of gravy. I was looking forward –'

'My granddaughter is upstairs, possessed by a demon. We can get more pies later, Mildred.' Hilda dipped a fresh ladle into the seething liquid. 'Feed the magic.'

Mildred quite literally sprang into action. With a jiggety-jig and a thrust of the hips, she held the pies aloft as she muttered words of incantation. 'Baker, baker, great pie maker, calm our potion, make it safer.'

Plop.

The chowder simmered gently, settled, then turned the rich, creamy hue of tomato soup.

'I think we done it, Hild. Looks gert lush. What now?'

Hilda consulted the recipe. 'Place thirteen large ladlefuls of broth into a baking tray and cook at the top of a preheated oven for thirteen minutes.'

★

The timer beeped. Hilda removed their creation from the oven, placed it on a breadboard in the centre of the kitchen table and removed her oven gloves.

Mildred sniffed it. 'Don't smell like no hex potion I ever seen.' She stood back and considered the thing in the tray. 'Don't look like one neither.'

Hilda could not disagree. During the baking process, the potion had turned a mushy-pea green and developed brown lumpy bits. It looked like a flapjack, the main ingredient of which was vomit.

'What we supposed to do with it?'

'According to Mistress Birdwhistle's directions, we have to

release the demon from the stasis spell and – '

'That ain't a good idea, Hild. Demons is sneaky buggers and that one up there ain't very nice. You heard what it said when it turned up.'

Hilda had. It had cussed and threatened with controlled ire, promising to inflict eternal pain on Emily's soul. The demon had also been eloquent in its blasphemy, which suggested intelligence. Thankfully, this wasn't their first demonic possession. They knew to act fast and cast a spell that would stun the demon long enough to complete a stasis hex. No wonder they were exhausted. They had performed more magic in the last day than they usually would in six months.

'We *have* to release the demon from the stasis hex, Mildred, and trick it into eating a slice of Baker's Zodiac. We'll be ready this time; we know what we're dealing with.'

They transferred their gaze to the steaming, baked thing. It had started to glow, and not in a good way. The aura accentuated the lumps in its skin.

'If we're supposed to get someone to eat it,' said Mildred, 'why does it look like nuclear cat puke?'

'If magic was easy, the unqualified could attempt it.'

'True, Hild. But sometimes... sometimes witchcraft gets right on me tits.'

Hilda's eyes fell on the kitchen's baking cupboard. Mildred had won the cup for Best Decorated Cake at Portishead's Summer Show seven years running.

'I bet you can make it look delicious.'

Mildred stared at the glowing Baker's Zodiac. It was sitting in a growing puddle of oily residue.

'Not sure there's enough icing in the world for that, Hild.'

'Come on, Mildred. Midnight is only an hour away. We're running out of time.'

IV

Hilda opened the bedroom door. Emily was floating again, her feet gently nudging the ceiling's lampshade.

'Is it time?' Hilda asked.

Mildred checked her watch. 'Almost midnight. It's time.'

Hilda waved her wand. The mist that surrounded Emily's body slowly swirled into the wand's tip. Her granddaughter dropped down onto the bed and lurched upright. Her face was still all over the place and her eyes shone like a shark's.

'Miserable bitches,' the demon muttered. Its cruel tone was out of place in the child's voice. 'This young body will pay for your insolence.' Its side-smile widened and opened Emily's face like a wound. 'Your fatuity led to this. I shall enjoy watching as your love turns to guilt and consumes you.'

Hilda clenched her dentures. 'It was a mistake.'

'That it was, old hag. And it will nourish me, for I feed on consequences, on guilt, on shame.'

Hilda took a deep breath. 'We have something to offer you in return for leaving Emily unharmed.'

The demon cocked Emily's head. 'A proposition? What could *you* possibly offer *me*?'

Mildred held a plate forward. On it was a beautifully iced... well, there was so much icing it was impossible to tell what.

'What is that?' The demon didn't sound impressed.

'Cake,' said Hilda.

The demon stood up. Emily's face began to rearrange itself. All her features found their rightful place, but her eyes... they were all pupil and shone red, like the bowels of hell. Grey mist seeped from her nose and clawed at the air.

'It's not just any cake,' said Hilda. 'A Cake of Life, prepared from Mistress Birdwhistle's recipe. An elixir of – '

'Thank you, for such a delicious feast.'

Hilda felt a sliver of hope.

'Oh, not that thing on the plate, hag. Your lies. They feed me, make me stronger. And now I feel your hate – a delicious dessert.' It laughed a laugh that wasn't a laugh. 'I will break this child in front of your eyes and feed on your anguish, for that is the most divine nectar of all.'

Hilda felt Mildred's hand on her shoulder.

'Speak to Emily, Hild.'

Mildred's wisdom seeped into Hilda. What did this *thing* know about divinity? She took a step forward. 'Emily,' she said. 'Can you hear me, my love?'

The demon recoiled as Hilda spoke. Emily's face began to twist. Her jaw dislocated, accompanied by hideous popping sounds. Hilda fought her emotions. This was an illusion; a trick to put her off. It was time to employ a different kind of magic. No spells or potions or ley lines or witchcraft. She focused on one thing.

'Emily, I need your help. You're the bravest little girl I know.'

The demon started to growl. Emily's right leg shot out horizontally and moved up the side of her body until it protruded from her armpit. Then it began to twist around in a slow circle.

'Look, bitch. Witness what I'm doing to this pathetic infant's body.'

Hilda closed her eyes.

'Think of your mother, Nanna Mildred... and me, your granny. Think of Grandad Harold and the fun you used to have with him, running in the woods at Ashton Court.'

Thinking of Harold gave Hilda more strength.

'It's my fault this thing possessed you, my mistake, for which I'm very sorry. I shouldn't have let you play that game, not here. But we can beat it, my love. I just need your help.'

The growling stopped. Hilda opened her eyes. Emily was looking at her – jaw and leg back where they should be – shivering and frightened. The demon's aura still gleamed in her eyes, but Emily's irises kept flickering from red to blue. Mildred was already holding the Baker's Zodiac forward.

'Emily, my love,' said Hilda. 'Please, take a bite of this. It's a medicine that will help you.'

The demon began to fight. Red flickered more than blue. Emily's hand reached out, pulled back, reached out again.

'We love you, sweet girl,' said Mildred.

'That we do,' said Hilda. 'More than anything.'

Droplets of sweat gathered on Emily's brow. One eye was red, the other blue. The demon was regaining its hold.

'You have a gift, Emily. I know you can feel it prickling in your mind. Let it creep through your body, over your skin, into your core. You'll feel its chemistry, burning and churning. The gift won't hurt you. It can't. It *is* you. Embrace it. Fight this thing. Banish it.'

Hilda picked up the Baker's Zodiac, cradled the back of Emily's head, and touched her lips with the food. 'A nibble is all it will take, sweetheart. You can do it, I know you can. I believe in you.'

Emily groaned, but not in pain. It was the groan of a young girl filled with determination, fight... and magic.

She bit down on the Zodiac, chewed and swallowed.

The glass in the bedroom window shattered. The door ripped off its hinges. Lightbulb fragments rained down from above. Hilda caught Emily and fell to her knees. They held each other tightly as a cluster of fireworks flashed and banged outside, their colours reflected in the broken glass.

V

A bell clanged and Mildred answered the door.

'Hello, Jan love. Come in out of the rain.'

'Hi, Aunty Mil. Sorry I'm a bit late. Traffic around the Cumberland Basin was chocka.'

'How was the nightshift?'

'You know how A&E gets on a weekend. I'm back on days next week, thank God.'

Hilda was sitting in her rocking chair, reading a book with Emily.

'Did you have fun, Em?' Janice asked.

'*So* much fun, Mummy. Can I sleep over again tonight?'

'Not tonight, love. School tomorrow.' Janice bent down, kissed Hilda on the cheek, and gave Emily a hug. 'Come on, time to go.'

'Have you got time for a coffee, Janice?'

'Sorry, Mum. I have to get home and start dinner.'

'Just a quick word then. It's important.'

Mildred grabbed Emily's hand. 'I almost forgot. We can't be sending you home without any cake now, can we?' She marched Emily towards the kitchen. 'That would be plain rude when I got a fresh-baked lemon drizzle in the larder with your name all over it.'

The kitchen door clicked shut.

'Sit, Janice, please,' said Hilda.

Janice perched on the edge of the sofa.

'Emily won't stop asking me questions. The more I avoid them, the more persistent she becomes. You weren't blessed with the gift, Janice, so you can't help her. Not like I'm able to. I'd like to spend more time with her, give her some guidance.'

'You know how I feel about that, Mum. I'd rather she did something… you know… safer. Something normal.'

Hilda reached out and took Janice's hand. 'So would I.

Really, I would. But she's drawn to the occult. It's part of who she is. A witch always finds a way to be a witch, no matter what anyone does to stop them. It's safer to respect Emily's choice and support her.'

'She asks about magic all the time at home too…' Janice squeezed Hilda's fingers. 'Just give me some time to think – to talk with her and make sure it's the right thing to do, OK?'

Emily charged back into the room with a bag in her hand. 'Look, Mummy, lemon drizzle, chocolate sponge *and* Welsh cakes.'

'Well, aren't you the luckiest little girl?' Janice took Emily's hand. 'Come on, we really have to get home. Have you got all your things, Em?'

Emily grabbed her bag from behind the door. 'See you soon, Granny. See you soon, Nanna Mil.'

Mildred gave her a hug and a kiss. 'Bye, love.'

'I'll call you, Mum,' said Janice.

The door had almost shut when Janice popped her head back in.

'Oh, by the way – the house next door to us is going on the market. You should come and take a look. It's old, but modernised. Practical, safe, well looked after. And you'd be right next door. It might make my decision easier.' Before Hilda could reply, Janice added, 'Just think about it.'

The door shut. Hilda's shoulders sagged and Mildred sank into an armchair.

'Bleedin' heck, Hild, what a weekend.'

'Language, Mildred.'

'After what we been through, I'm allowed a swear. I ain't puttin' nothin' in the swear jar neither. And I'll tell you another thing.'

'Oh, will you?'

'Yes, I will. Next time Emily comes over, no matter how much she asks, we ain't playing with that damned Ouija board.

All those memory alterin' spells on the little-un have knackered us out.'

'We had to, Mildred. She's too young to – '

'I know, Hild, I just don't like it is all. And then… then we had to pretend like it didn't happen.' She held up trembling hands. 'I'm a quiverin' wreck.'

'I'm sorry, Mildred. She's so interested in witchcraft… I wanted to be there for her. I just went about it all wrong. It was stupid of me. Never again, I promise.'

Mildred sighed and looked around the room. 'So, where's it to?'

'What?'

'The Ouija board. You didn't let our Em take it home, did you?'

Hilda picked up her knitting and started to purl stitch. 'Of course not.'

'So, what you done with it?'

'Used it to start the fire.'

Mildred chuckled. 'Good call.'

Hilda knitted for a while, then –

'What do you think about Janice's idea, Mildred? To look at her neighbour's house.'

Mildred sipped her tea. 'Not a big fan of modernised houses. Ain't got no character. Look alright on the outside, disappointing on the inside. Like a doughnut with no jam. Besides, I like it here.'

'How would you feel about living here alone?'

'You really considering Jan's idea, huh?'

Hilda was exhausted. She loved her vocation, but the toll it took on her… Her decision about playing with the Ouija board proved her judgement was failing. Something had to change.

'I'm approaching eighty, Mildred. I want to spend more time with my family.'

'I am family.' Mildred sounded dejected.

'That's not what I mean.' Hilda picked up a framed picture of her husband from beside her chair. 'I keep thinking about Harold, how he put off retiring and passed before we could spend quality time together. I don't want to make the same mistake. If I lived nearer, I could see Emily all the time and guide her without having to worry. Houses in the city don't stand on magical ground.'

'Except those cottages at Blaise Hamlet. Oh, and then there's them ones round Arnos Vale Cemetery. And – '

'OK, *most* of them don't.'

Mildred's expression softened. 'Suppose Totterdown is quite nice. Colourful terraces. Artistic, bohemian. They do that Front Room Arts Trail thing. Quite like that.'

'You just like nosing around other people's houses.'

'I do not,' snapped Mildred. 'It's the art I likes.'

Hilda raised an eyebrow.

'Look, Totterdown's nice, but it ain't for me.' Mildred slurped her tea. 'I know that from all my nosin'.'

Hilda knitted another row.

'What about witching?' Mildred asked.

'I'll never stop being a witch. I can't, you know that.'

'But?'

Hilda wiped her nose. 'I'd dabble, rather than practice the art. Janice lives walking distance from Arnos Vale, so if I needed to be somewhere enchanted I could get there easily. Use it to teach Emily.'

'Would you help me out, until I train an apprentice? I can't go collecting them unmentionable bull fluids on me own now, can I?'

'Of course I'd help, whenever you needed me.'

Mildred handed Hilda the phone. 'Call Jan and ask her to book a viewing. I'll go with you.'

Hilda had been expecting more of a fight.

'You're not angry?'

Mildred had moisture in her eyes. 'I been expecting it, Hild. I'm a witch too, you know.'

As Hilda lifted the phone's receiver, a feeling of contentment fluttered in her stomach. *Hilda Jane Beauchamp, Witch. Retired.*

Well, mostly.

Going Down Brean

Rebecca Watts

MAGGIE WAS HUNCHED ON the mud in the back garden, sifting grit through her dusty fingers.

'Beach mission tomorrow,' she commented to Kieran who was perched on his football next to her. 'You can come if you want.'

'You'd have to accept Jesus as your Lord and Saviour – wouldn't he?' Elsa called from the back step. 'Maggie has.'

'No, I have not.'

'Yeah, she has, Kieran. She's going to get a dunk in the great big bath.'

'Shut up, Elsa. I only go because you get to go on trips,' she said.

'Do you have to sing and that?' Kieran asked.

'Yeah, Maggie knows all the songs, don't you Maggie?' said Elsa. 'Come on and celebrate.'

Maggie kicked out at Elsa, striking her on the shin. She suppressed the urge to kick her again as Elsa retreated back to the step, her eyes full of tears.

'Some people sing,' Maggie told him. 'But you don't have

to, not if you don't want. You can just run off and play on the sand.'

'As long as you're back at the bus by four. Isn't it Maggie?' Elsa remembered.

'Yeah,' Maggie, replied, more gently now. 'We can just play football.'

'And there's a shop to buy stuff,' said Elsa. 'That's where I got these jelly shoes.' She poked her foot towards Kieran.

'Yeah, alright,' said Kieran. 'Do I have to put my name down?'

'Ours are down already,' said Elsa as she jumped on the spot excitedly.

'If you get there early you'll probably get on.'

'Alright,' Kieran stood and flicked the ball into his hands, 'see you in the morning.'

'Bring your ball, Kier,' Maggie shouted after him.

'Yeah.' He did not turn back as he waved.

Maggie was woken by Elsa the following morning. She opened her eyes and saw her sister already dressed in a felt-tip dappled yellow t-shirt and blue shorts, her head covered with a large, purple sun hat.

'I've got my swimming costume on already Maggie,' Elsa said and lifted up her t-shirt to show her glossy pink swimsuit tight against her tubby belly. Maggie groaned and tunnelled under the duvet.

'Does six pounds mean three pounds each, Maggie?' Elsa's muffled voice reached her.

'Yeah.'

'We've got three pounds each then. You don't have to look after mine this year. I can look after it myself.'

Maggie peeked out and saw her own red purse dangling from a thin white rope around Elsa's neck, its popper clipped shut and the name 'Margaret' printed in white letters on the front.

'She left a note as well Maggie. What does it say?'

Maggie heaved herself up to look.

'Have a great day. Love Mum.' She fell back on to her pillow and looked at her watch. 'It's only 6.20, Else. The bus doesn't leave 'til ten.'

'But what time will we have to leave here?'

'About ten to ten.'

'How long's that?'

'Another three and a half hours.'

'Oh, I'll just go and wait then,' Elsa said as she backed out of the room.

They were an hour early and there were already three before them – Carly Westlake, Janine Walsh and Patrick Maxwell. Maggie knew they couldn't have their names down. They hadn't been to church since the Easter Egg service. At quarter to ten Maggie counted 28 children waiting. They stood close to the kerb, desperately trying to judge which direction the Reverend and the minibus would arrive from. Elsa no longer swung her purse so brightly and her cheeks were pinched tight. Maggie wanted to reassure her but she didn't. She knew the minibus only seated fifteen, tops. Hannah, Ruth, Joshua and Joseph, whose mums all did the teas on a Sunday, didn't arrive until ten to ten and they sat nonchalantly on the wall behind the jostling throng, confidently assured of their place. There was another boy with them who hadn't been going to church long, who they called PJ. At first, Maggie had been unsure which row of the church he belonged to until she found out it stood for Peter John. Double the Christian name. He automatically joined the front pew on Sundays.

The crowd surged forward when the minibus arrived and

they crammed tight against it, trying, in vain, to open the sliding door. Maggie felt anxious to join them but decided to stick close to PJ and the others who remained unconcerned on the wall. The Reverend was trapped in the driver's seat and flapped his clipboard in an attempt to bat them away. He wound down the window and was met with the full shock of their appeals.

'Sir, sir,' they cried.

'I was christened up the other church, sir.'

'Carly can't come so she said I could have her place.'

'But I'm here,' Carly called from behind.

'Right. Mind out of the way, the lot of you,' a raging voice shouted from the back.

Maggie immediately recognised Rodney Chubb's mum who strode through, in blue and white deck shoes. Rodney was already on the minibus.

'I'm the 'elper on this 'ere trip,' she bellowed. 'And you've all got to listen to me. Give I that.' She thrust a tattooed arm towards the Reverend and prised the clipboard from his reluctant hand. 'None of you is getting on, unless I says so. Right. You,' Mrs Chubb signalled to Joshua.

'Joshua Mundy.'

'Right, on you get,' she made space for him to squeeze through.

Hannah, Ruth, PJ and Joseph were permitted to board next.

'You,' Mrs Chubb demanded as Elsa silently gulped air.

'She's Elsa,' Maggie spoke for her, 'Elsa Tanner, and I'm her sister Maggie.'

'They're both definitely down,' the Reverend explained as he smiled at them.

'This is Kieran, sir,' Maggie tried. 'Our mum's looking after him today. So he has to come. Otherwise he'll have to wait on the wall until we get back.'

'That's not fair,' the others screeched.

'I really think we should make space,' the Reverend conceded. 'All the children with their names down are on.'

That was all the invitation Maggie, Elsa and Kieran needed to scramble aboard. They had to sit with their legs bent and their feet resting against the church banner and the Reverend's guitar that was lying across the floor.

There were just three seats left and Carly, Janine and Patrick were approved to clamber on too.

'Right. That's it. We're full.' Mrs Chubb firmly slid the door shut. The disappointed children milled around the bus and peered through the window.

'What about that seat there?'

'That's for the sandwiches and that,' Mrs Chubb replied and dumped a box of sandwiches and two large bottles of squash on it.

'Bleedin' fuckers,' Mrs Chubb tutted to the Reverend as they struggled into the front and he pulled out the choke.

'You might have to help me with the directions Mrs Chubb,' said the Reverend.

'Ain't you never been down Brean before?' she asked him disbelievingly.

'Well, no, I can't say I have.'

'Oh, it's blimmin' great down there, ain't it kids?'

'Yeah,' they all called from the back.

The Reverend joined the stampede of traffic on the Portway. At the roundabout they drove past the usual turning for the back-to-back terraces of Avonmouth and the dock gates and instead made for the large overhead signs marking routes to The North and The South.

'M5 South, drive.' Mrs Chubb called.

'We're really going Maggie. We're really going,' Elsa bounced in her seat beside her.

They took the slip road that led south and stayed in the

slowest lane, carried along by two juggernauts belching at front and back. Their seats juddered as the minibus reached for the crest of the motorway bridge, the lorry behind threatening to flatten and outrun them.

'Lean forward you lot.' Mrs Chubb directed and thrust her body towards the dashboard.

'Mrs Chubb,' the Reverend reddened uncomfortably, 'I really don't think that…'

'What do you think I am? Soft in the 'ead? Just a bit of a laugh for them ain't it?'

Her thumb jerked to the children all bent double as they willed the minibus forward. Over the bridge Maggie could see the river, receded to a trickle on oozing mud banks and the cranes of the docks, unmanned and motionless. Maggie's eyes were scorched as she stared at the roof-tops of thousands of cars, glimmering in the sun, unloaded, parked up and unsold.

'Gordano Services, there look Rev,' Mrs Chubb pointed. 'Shouldn't really stop yet, should we?' she asked, half-hoping.

'Well, I don't think we've gone a mile yet.'

'Best get down there and make the most of the beach. Can do the services anytime.'

A right turn took them onto a single track lane that ran straight as far as Maggie could see. On one side static caravans cascaded down a steep bank and hundreds more stretched along a level plain on the other. A solitary woman washed down the windows of one. Grains of sand thinly coated the track and swirled up towards the bus.

'That's sand, Maggie.' Elsa gripped the seat in front excitedly. 'Almost there.' They passed the wooden entrance to the Sunny Glades Holiday Park offering *Manilow Magicke Tonite*. They continued until the ranks of caravans were replaced with the concrete wall of the car park.

'In 'ere, Rev.'

'Are you sure?' The Reverend frowned as he read the large

sign in cautionary red and yellow. 'Dangerous sinking sand and mud at low tide.'

'Yeah, this is it, ain't it kids.'

The Reverend inched the minibus into the car park. A small shack was huddled in the corner, inflated dolphins and rubber rings tethered to its corrugated iron flat roof. They began to click themselves free of their seat belts but Mrs Chubb stopped them.

'None of you is getting out 'til I says so. Now. Just listen to me. Don't go too far. Got to see me and the Reverend. Ain't that right?'

'What time's the sandwiches?' Patrick shouted.

'At dinner time. We'll shout you over, won't we, Rev. Then spreading the Word and the bus back after that.'

Maggie looked down at Elsa who gingerly manoeuvred her arms out of the sleeves of her t-shirt in preparation. Mrs Chubb slid open the door and they rushed out, Elsa leading the way down the steps that led onto the beach. She tore off her t-shirt, skipped out of her shorts and discarded them in a straggly heap while she charged, twirled and hop-scotched into the vast expanse of sand. Maggie screwed her eyes to take in the huge dank, yellow beach, broken by exposed islands of families huddled behind billowing windbreaks. An ice-cream van was parked some way off, the man inside reading a newspaper. Beyond it, the sand darkened to a brown sludge, leftovers from the river that now lapped miles in the distance. Still further again, clouds shifted and scurried over land that Maggie knew was another country, Wales.

Kieran whacked his football to soar high over the sand. It was pummelled mid-flight and landed far beyond from where he had intended. Maggie raced after it and thrust it back to him. Elsa settled cross-legged and started to scoop out a hole in the sand.

Mrs Chubb dragged two hired deck chairs back from the

shop, handed one to the Reverend and sank herself down. Carly performed a run of five perfect cartwheels to PJ and Hannah. Kieran flapped his arms towards Maggie's direction and tunnelled his hands around his straining mouth, but she could not make out what he was hollering. He pointed in the direction of the car park but gave up and ran to her, dribbling the football at his feet.

'Shall we go to the shop?' he panted.

'Yeah alright. We'd better get Elsa.'

As Maggie approached she noticed that her feet were buried under two rounded mounds of sand.

'We're going to the shop, Else.'

'Oh,' Elsa looked down in the direction of her feet uncertainly, not wanting to disturb the carefully smoothed surface concealing them. 'Can you say, "Where are your feet?" Maggie?'

'What?' she replied impatiently.

'Pretend you don't know where my feet are and say, "I wonder where they could be?" and then I could surprise you,' she giggled.

'You're too old for that, Else.'

'Please, just once.'

'No. If you're coming, you need to come now.' Maggie turned and headed for the car park. Elsa ruptured the sand and stamped on it before hurrying to catch them up. Maggie felt guilty when she saw Elsa regard her anxiously and she immediately regretted not doing as she had asked.

'I'll do it when we get back,' she gently offered.

'What?'

'That thing with your feet. I'll do it when we get back. You can bury them again.'

'It doesn't matter now.' Elsa shrugged and trotted ahead.

They flinched across the car park in bare, sandy feet. The contents of the shop spilled outside, silver foil windmills spinning upright in plastic ice-cream containers. There were fort-shaped buckets for sandcastles in marble blue and red and smaller, circular buckets in yellow. Next to them were two different sorts of spade. The more expensive ones had smooth wooden handles and strong metal shovels and the cheaper ones were made of plastic. More ice-cream boxes were filled to the brim with flip-flops and jelly shoes, black pen on the side marking the size.

Elsa eyed a pink rubber ring shifting on the roof.

'How much is that, Maggie?'

'£1.99.'

'Can I have it?'

'What for? You won't be able to go in the water, it's filthy.'

'Just to wear.'

'Let's have a look at what else there is. You might change your mind.'

Kieran was at a dustbin filled with plastic footballs. He took out a few and expertly prodded and bounced them.

'Any good?' Maggie asked.

'Nah, not really. See what's inside first.'

It was dark inside the shop, the window was blocked by a box filled with wicker beach mats and windbreaks, and it took a few seconds for Maggie's eyes to adjust. Along one wall were sticks of chunky, hard, pink rock with names embedded through them. There were flat, red lollipops and full fried breakfasts of sugary sweets covered in cling-film on paper plates. Baskets of shells displayed rigid crusty starfish and other shells smooth and coiled. Kieran was holding a packet of Red Arrow Acrobatic Gliders.

'They do loop the loops and everything when you've put them together.'

Maggie sorted through cardboard boxes of yo-yos, hard bouncing balls and green plastic snakes that unsteadily wriggled beyond her. She picked up a bottle of bubbles and tried to steer the single ball-bearing through a tiny maze set in its lid. She silently dismissed the bat and balls whose rackets boomed when you hit them and the cricket sets made from pale, sickly wood. She was tempted by the kites, neatly folded in packets, but remembered how quickly the thin cotton had tangled when she tried to launch one before.

She was staring at bags of marbles in mesh netting when she noticed something she was certain had not been there last year. The Funnyman Joke Stand. She tripped over a stray foot pump in her urgency to reach it and gazed at the small packets of practical jokes. Maggie supposed they were like the ones that Betty and Alicia from Malory Towers sent away to a special catalogue for. She calculated that she had enough for two and an ice cream for later. On the top rack she spotted a pot labelled 'Invisible Ink'. Maggie thought it would be perfect for if she was ever held prisoner and her captors forced her to write a letter calling for a ransom. She would be able to write another in the invisible ink to warn people of her plight. Her mind was made up. She would buy the invisible ink and the bendy pencil. Kieran had added a bouncy ball to his aeroplane.

'Oh, wicked,' he exclaimed as he saw the 'Nail through Finger' on the joke stand and swapped it for the bouncy ball.

'Have you decided, Else?' Maggie asked.

'I could have a little think and come back later,' she suggested hopefully.

'You'd better get it now. Otherwise, there won't be much time for the beach.'

'I'll get the rubber ring and a fishing net then.'

'You won't be able to use them.'

'Yes, I will, I'll pretend.'

'Elsa...' Maggie warned.

'It's my money,' Elsa tried desperately. 'I'll tell Mum.'

'Alright,' Maggie conceded and Elsa beamed.

The man calculated how much they owed him, writing on

a paper bag with a bitten biro, his cigarette slouched in the corner of his mouth. Their coins were dropped into a metal box and with fumbling fingers he handed them their change.

'Can we have the rubber ring on the roof, please?'

He grunted and squeezed himself out from behind the counter. As he shambled out he picked up a hook attached to a long pole and dragged the pink ring down from the roof. He added air from the electric pump humming by the door before handing it to Elsa, who put it over her head and hugged it to her waist.

'And a fishing net, please,' Elsa asked.

'Colour?'

'A pink one, please.'

He untangled one of the whittled bamboo canes against the wall and Elsa grasped it to her and they headed back to the beach, satisfied.

'Quick Maggie,' Elsa turned to call. 'Sandwiches.' They ran to join the others who were eagerly clustered at the foot of Mrs Chubb's deck chair.

'Sit down, the lot of you,' Mrs Chubb slapped away their hunting fingers. 'There's jam or chocolate spread. Don't think you're just 'avin chocolate spread. You'll all get one of each.'

She twirled open the Sunblest bags the sandwiches had been packed in and Maggie was handed two halves, the white bread moist and stretchy and imprinted with the tips of Mrs Chubb's fingers. Maggie caught a strand of hair in her first bite and tugged it out through her mouthful. Despite meticulously brushing her hands free of sand, her teeth still crunched as she chewed. Mrs Chubb lifted the bottle of watery squash and held it between her thighs as she twisted off the lid. She swapped the bottle for a stack of white plastic cups and poured them half-full and handed one to each of them. Maggie's was gone in two gulps. There were Penguins for afters. They had begun to melt in the heat and Maggie stuffed hers into her mouth in one, the chocolate coating her teeth.

Maggie and Kieran bolted free when the Reverend started to tune up his guitar and ran in zigzags across the sand until their burst of revolt was spent. They gasped for breath together and Kieran pulled out the aeroplane from his pocket and feverishly ripped off its vacuum-packed wrapper. He hastily pulled the wings through the slit in its body and Maggie retrieved the tiny propeller that had fallen into the sand. He pulled his arm back as far as he could reach before catapulting it forward and releasing the plane to soar, spin and float through the sky. The proper Christians were standing around the Reverend's guitar singing 'Father Abraham'. Elsa settled her rubber ring on the sand and knelt outside its perimeter and started to dig a hole in the centre. As her hands dug deeper, the sand became wetter and she plucked her fishing net, scooped it down into the puddle and swung it skyward.

'A fish, a fish, a fish,' Elsa yelled.

'Is it a big one, Else?' Maggie asked.

'Shark,' she replied before plunging her net back down into the soggy ferment.

Maggie felt the remaining coins jangling in her pocket and remembered ice-cream. She called to Elsa and Kieran and pointed towards the van. The man was sitting in the driver's seat, his feet resting on the dashboard, but as they approached he rose and bent towards them through the window. As Maggie surveyed the faded, discoloured stickers stuck to the inside of the window she could hear the generator whirring. She dismissed the lollies – cola, cider, orange, lemonade, Zooms and strawberry mivvis. Cornets came in three sizes small, medium or large with flakes for ninety-nines fifteen pence extra.

'I'll have a Zoom please,' Elsa decided first. The man turned and slid open the silver lid of the flat-topped freezer and reached into a cardboard box and handed her one. There were crystals of ice frozen around the bottom and she had to use all her puff to inflate the wrapper and pull the lolly free. Kieran chose a medium cornet without a flake and Maggie did the same. They watched admiringly as the man held the two empty cones in one hand and expertly spiralled soft ice-cream into each.

'Strawberry sauce?' he asked.

'Is it extra?'

'Nah, you're alright.' They nodded as he squirted a trail of red syrup on both.

Mrs Chubb hollered them back at four. Elsa refused to put her clothes back on and Maggie gathered them in her arms. They disregarded the buckles and laces of their shoes, flattened their heels and scuffed their way back to the minibus. The seats were hot and sticky and they had to raise their legs to avoid them burning on the metal frame.

Maggie's skin felt tight and prickled with the sun and her hair briskly tangled. As the van started to shift away, the breeze from an open window budded goose bumps on her arm. At the church Kieran went one way and Maggie and Elsa the other. Elsa trooped tiredly, the rubber ring falling diagonally across her shoulder, and dragged her fishing net caked with sand. As they neared home, Elsa revived and shouted through the letter box.

'Mum, it's us.'

Nan opened the door. 'Hello my lovers, I was just saying to your mother…'

Elsa burst through to Mum who was ironing in the corner.

'Fishing rod, Mum, look and a rubber ring.' Elsa held both up and dislodged sand onto the carpet. 'We saw the seaside and had a jam sandwich for dinner, the Reverend preached the Word and Mrs Chubb called us bleedin' fuckers.'

Malago Days

K.M. Elkes

SUPPOSE YOU WERE A stranger discovering the Malago river for the first time – perhaps because you had taken a wrong turn on the way to the city centre, or were a nervous child looking for a bully-avoiding shortcut, or one of those flaneurs from Clifton crossing the DMZ of the New Cut to explore Bristol's southern reaches – and suppose you paused for a moment to watch the Malago's modest flow, a flow that starts down the long green hill from Dundry, before meandering through Withywood, Hartcliffe and Bedminster, past back gardens and light industrial estates, round dams of tyres and shopping trolleys, along the perimeter of the old gasworks and auto suppliers and tiling contractors and the yards of factories where workers gather to smoke and toss their stubs into the foamy water, beyond warehouses and slivers of parks and the underworld stretches of blacked-out culverts; then you might be tempted to conclude that the Malago is an unremarkable river in an unremarkable corner of the city.

It's not an outlandish deduction. The surrounding streets have suffered casualties over the years. The old library and school closed a while back. Half a dozen pubs have gone the way of boarded windows and silent taps. All around are the ghosts of corner shops converted into flats and closed down hairdressing salons, their window posters of glum hair models bleached to a pale, pale blue.

And yet, like the Malago itself, appearances can be deceptive. Take the Headley Café, where the day starts with Rose Tizzard, sole proprietor, flipping the sign from Closed to Open at 7am sharp, then taking her station behind the counter, its surface already polished to a monumental shine.

Our Rose is a smart woman of wedged heels and immaculate nails. Of roundness and pearl earrings and one eyebrow held a little higher than the other. Rose sends out to the world a certain knowing sassiness, though on her 'bad' days she has squatted by the plug sockets in her bedroom, scared witless that all the electricity will leak out, and sometimes at night she lies awake scooping the air to her ears for its secret sounds.

Five minutes she waits before Billy Stenner arrives, as he has done every weekday for longer than either of them can bear to remember.

'Alright, Rose, love. Loaf-baker of a day out there already.'

The voice is clotted with tobacco and sweetened by a hint of Somerset. Not an old man, Billy, but deep enough into middle age to be measuring its end. The demise of the pub across from the café was a godsend to his liver. Now he survives on Rose's pitch-thick tea. He reckons himself a raconteur with a handful of decent yarns but is not immune to the 3am bell toll of gloom.

There's a dent in the seat at the window table, a depression worried into the fabric where Billy takes daily residence. As the smell of bacon rises from Rose's pan, he reaches up and furtively eases down the blind.

'You can keep your hands off that,' says Rose, without turning around. 'Customers will think we're closed.'

'You know the door's wide open, don't you? I'm not one of them lizards that needs warming.'

'I'll not tell 'ee again,' says Rose. It is her stern voice, so Billy complies.

After breakfast, he clicks his pen for the Cryptic. Most days he scuppers it easily enough, reading out clues to Rose who ponders while he's already writing them in. Then he reads the paper, looks out onto the street, watches Rose rearranging stock, making lists, always moving.

When the paper is done, Billy pulls out a small, ancient radio from his jacket pocket, the kind with a greasy, off-white earpiece that reminds him of a tooth. If he tunes it carefully, he can find the local station and keep up with the news. Plans for a crackdown on teenage drinking. A woman in Portishead celebrating her 101st birthday. A lorry that's shed its load causing tailbacks out by Aztec West. It's enough, just, to remind him of a wider world, though he feels in the static crackle of the airwaves a separation from it all.

★

Late morning, four lads bundle through the door. They are hot with noise, sniffing and coughing as they check the menu board. They wear fluorescent yellow tabards over bare chests, thudding boots and trousers starched with grime. They carry hard hats.

'Let me guess,' says Billy. 'You lot are scaffolders, am I right?'

They turn. One has a gold hoop looped through his eyebrow. He can't be more than eighteen.

'You'll like this,' says Billy, who shifts round in his chair and rolls up a trouser leg. The skin is corrugated where a scar runs the length of his shin.

'Like a Meccano set in there. Sixteen pieces of metal. Came off me motorbike didn't I.'

The young men nod and smile, but quickly turn away. Billy feels wetted by a dab of pity that makes his stomach turn.

'Ah well,' he says, quietly. 'Happened a long time ago, anyways.'

While they place their orders and wait, Billy folds his newspaper and considers them, the already leathered hands, the sunburnt necks, the thumbs that could persuade a nail into a wall. He senses the ease with which they would throw themselves around the scaffold towers, fearless of height. The daring, loose-limbed throb of life in them.

He remembers himself at the same age. A young, eager Billy who often went down to the Floating Harbour to see the ships, and the men who worked them, in the dying days of the docks. This Billy dreamed of being carried by the tide down the Avon, out into the Bristol Channel and away, elsewhere, gone. His dad was a merchant seaman, rarely home and one day never home again. Billy recollects the smell of oil and dust from his father's clothes and the blue, blurred lines of his tattoos – a knotted rope, a nautical star, three swallows flying across his shoulders. But young Billy's ambition to earn his own tattoos curdled through the years into a comfortable rhythm of weekends on the lash and weekdays making ends meet. His desire to ride out on the tide reduced to a trickle that in time disappeared like the Malago into its dark culverts.

Billy knows that lads like the scaffolders don't yet suffer this curse of reflection. Not for them the onset of a sudden, inexplicable fear whenever the wind rattles through a high garden fence, nor when walking by the river in the early hours and seeing a fox nose through a rubbish sack before it stops, looks, then carries on unperturbed. No tight-chested desire to weep at a pair of shoes slung over a telephone wire by their laces, moving gently, taking baby steps. No sitting in a café suckling a daily drop of optimism from the sole proprietor, wondering where the years went. He wants to get up and shake these young men's hands, to quash his jealousy of their purpose. But he stays where he is. Of course he does.

Rose is natural with them. The men nod and laugh with her as they reach into the clear-fronted fridge to pull out drink cans and sandwiches wrapped in greaseproof paper. They flirt, though she could be a mother to them all. When one of them lets slip a 'fuck', she tuts and they all quieten.

There had been a moment a few summers back with Rose, when he thought the course of his life might just shift after all. A long night down the pub. An unexpected clutch on the steps of the café. An invite upstairs. Billy was struck by the smell of Rose's flat — cooked food, perfume, a little unaired. Her bedroom was buttered in yellow light from a street lamp. She said: 'So then…' and held him to her mouth like a good, long drink. When she undressed, he saw a narrow zip of raised skin on her stomach, the closed pocket of an appendectomy scar, and on both breasts puckered seams where her nipples should have been.

'Left them up Southmead Oncology Unit, if you was wondering,' said Rose.

There was a comfortable elegance in her plump, patched-upness, a life lived in a way that Billy admired. She took him in her mouth while her cat yawned beneath the clothes airer. He stared at the ceiling, its cracks and lines visible beneath a thin wash of magnolia paint and wondered what it would be like to trace journeys across them each night with Rose. Later, the streetlight softened her into one of those old film stars she loved so much.

When he left later that night, she kissed him like she meant it. But there had never been a repeat. He treasures her kindness and patience and friendship too much to ever mention it. But he fears that the happiness of that night was also the moment when he scoured out the very last of his passion.

After the scaffolders leave, he hears them down the street, a roar of laughter like an engine starting up as they turn the corner. He scratches and mutters until Rose walks over with a tea he hasn't asked for. And while it steams and settles and cools, the hands of the old clock on the café wall quiver their way through the long minutes and the street outside resumes its familiar face.

*

Most days this same old, same old, would drift through lunchtime and the unspooling afternoon – beyond Billy's excursions to the doorway for a stretch and a smoke, beyond a few customers popping in, beyond Rose, never idle, calling out ideas: 'What's your take on iced coffee?' 'How about a themed food day?' 'Could you see this place as an intimate music venue?'

But today, when Billy braves the doorway heat, when he thinks, the way he often does, of life running silently somewhere out of sight like the Malago itself, while he looks down the whole empty, aching length of the street, he sees an angel.

'What's this then?' he says out loud.

This is a woman in a silver dress, iridescent in the heat shimmer. This is a pair of glittering wings on her back, spilling sunlight. This is a face turned away from the bus stop timetable, to take in one end of the street, then the other. This is a pair of dark eyes looking at him, then walking his way. This is what this is.

Billy trots back to his seat as the angel approaches, tarries outside the door, then enters in a hurry of light. With her comes a wafted scent of perfume and stale alcohol. She walks the length of the café and back again, looks at the menu board, at the cakes on the counter under their glass cover, pulls out a chair at a table near the back then replaces it, finds another near the door, hesitates, turns, then finally sits. It is as though a wild bird has flown into the café and flapped around the place before landing. When Billy allows himself a glance, he sees the wings across her shoulders are homemade, tin-foiled and a little tattered.

He remembers, again, a younger, more carefree version of himself. A Billy who sped on his motorbike along the arrow-straight lanes of the Somerset Levels, who sat on the banks of the Malago in Manor Woods Valley listening to the gleeful tumble of water over rocks, scanning the trees for the dart and dash of kingfishers. A Billy who would not have hesitated to talk to angels with ruined wings, curious for their story.

But older Billy remains mute while the angel plucks a mobile phone from her handbag, checks it, puts it down, then picks it up and checks it again. It is only when she looks straight at him and nods that he finds his words.

'I reckon you've ended up in the wrong place here, love.'

When she smiles, there is a hint of shadow to it: 'No surprise there. I seem to make a habit of that.'

Her accent is not local, the way she speaks too clipped and nimble, but the voice is strong and clear.

'Out partying, was you? Fancy dress. Angels and devils and all that.'

'How did you know,' she says, and gives her wings a shake. 'It was a birthday party for a friend of my… what should I call him… my significant other. Yes, that's about right.'

Rose returns from the kitchen. When she sees the angel, she runs a tea towel through her fingers, and for a single glistening moment the tip of her tongue peeks from between her lips just as when she considers the crossword clues.

'Alright, love? The heat that sun's giving off, I expect you'll want a drink,' she says. 'Maybe a bite to eat?'

The angel nods and Rose puts on the kettle, hasn't even asked what she wants. Rose knows. Rose always knows.

The angel looks around the café, which is doing its best in the hard light. She is not quite as young as Billy first thought. There is a cleat between her eyebrows, a mix of frown and laughter lines that graph the expression of her face. Billy is eager to unfold the mystery of how the angel got from where she was, to where she is now. But before he can dredge up another question, she speaks again, as if she already knows what he wants to ask.

'I left the party. There was, I think, too much devil and not enough angel. I didn't know where to go, until I found this little river and followed it, all the way upstream to here.'

Rose brings out a drink and a sandwich for the angel, who pecks eagerly at it. After each mouthful she looks through the window to the white heat outside, then down at her plate again. When she is finished, she eases back her chair, stands and goes to the doorway, gazing out at the street. Despite the torpor of the midday sun, Billy feels as though something in the day is winding tight.

'You expecting someone,' says Rose eventually. It sounds like a question, but isn't.

'I'm sure it won't be too long,' says the angel. 'It's predictable as rain.'

'Your significant other?' asks Billy.

The angel comes back from the doorway, sits, pushes the empty plate and her cup aside and unhitches the wings from around her shoulders, laying them carefully on the table where they settle into a glittering mess.

'My significant other,' she says, 'is very good at games of hide-and-seek.'

She stretches her arms out across the table and lays her head flat. Without the wings he can see, above the scooped back of her dress, a tattoo covering her shoulders, though her skin looks too delicate for the needle and ink. Her back is a forest, bright with trees and wildflowers and birds. When she moves the whole scene comes to life in glossy greens and reds, yellows and blues, birds he wished he knew the names for perched and ready to fly from the branches that wrap and curve around her.

'You like it?' she says.

'I do, though that needle must have felt like a woodpecker's beak by the end.' Billy thinks of his dad's roughly drawn tattoos, and how he rolled up his sleeves to reveal them anyway, to show the world that he had been among it. 'What I reckon with tattoos is you never know how it's going to turn out until it's too late to change. That's the risk, see. But maybe some things are worth that risk and a bit of suffering besides, for how it turns out.'

When Billy says this, Rose stops polishing the cupboard doors behind the counter for a moment and looks at him, her one raised eyebrow raised a little further.

'All I know is it definitely brings a bit of colour to the place, love,' she says.

The angel lifts her head: 'But this is a good place. I like it. I want my own business, like you, one day.'

'Doing what then?' asks Billy.

The girl shakes her head: 'Ah no. You'd laugh. To say it out loud sounds such a stupid thing. A silly dream.'

'Try us,' says Rose.

'There's no shame in having a bit of ambition,' says Billy, which makes Rose's eyebrow twitch again.

'I want to buy an orchard, back where I grew up. I want to be the first person there to make cider, just like you have here!' She snorts and laughs and blushes, holds her face in her hands for a moment. 'It's crazy, right? But my grandfather had apple trees on his little farm when I was a child. I used to play under them and later he showed me how much to water them, and how to prune them and the best time to pick the apples and how to store them. So, yes, my silly little dream. An apple orchard in the village where I spent my summers. And cider to sell at the market. And a place to sit and watch things grow, in peace.'

It doesn't sound a stupid idea to Billy, but right – the smell of ripeness, the promise of something warm and beautiful. And though he doesn't know it yet, it is this small moment on this singular afternoon that will stay with Billy till the end of him, when most other memories have faded. He will taste a sweet sharpness in his mouth and remember the sad, beautiful angel with birds that fluttered across her as she laughed. And he will remember that the café transformed for a short time into something beyond itself. It will be a cupped handful of cool water to his face. A punch to his heart.

They talk on, the three of them, deep into the afternoon's stillness. Billy unwraps his old, surefooted anecdotes. But he listens too, as the angel tells them about her grandfather, their village, the country she is from, and all the many places she has been. Rose brings cups of tea and cakes and chats about the café, the street, her many plans for the future. And all the while she runs a finger round the tattered edges of her wings lying on the table between them, trying to smooth down the creases.

They talk on, while the shadows curve and lengthen, and on, until the angel's phone stirs like a waking wasp. She slides the green answer button across the screen and puts it to her ear.

'I did,' she says.

'I know,' she says.

'Don't start,' she says.

'I suppose,' she says.

'I will,' she says.

There is a long silence before the angel clicks off the phone and lays it carefully on the table. Then she picks up her wings, lowers them over her shoulders, and tightens the straps that hold them in place.

'Time's up,' she says, so quietly Billy barely catches it. And when she smiles at both of them again, it's a smile of someone already moving on.

'I need to pay,' says the angel.

'You'll do no such thing,' says Rose.

Though the day is bright and the café and the street look as they have always done, there is static fizz to the air. He wants to tell the angel before she goes something that will stay with her from this moment, like a bright coin in her purse that she might not spend too fast. But before he can think of any grand wisdom, he sees a car pull up outside, dark-windowed and gleaming, sleek as a panther. It sits and pants quietly in the heat. Nobody gets out.

'That's for me,' says the angel.

'Listen love,' says Billy. 'You don't have to go anywhere you don't want.'

'We can let you out the back door if need be,' says Rose.

'I'll go and have a word, just you let me know,' says Billy, sucking in his gut.

'No, please. It's not what you're thinking. Not that. It's just…' the angel waves her hand at the door and the world beyond: 'I suppose it's what you said, about the tattoo that's still being done.'

Billy nods. He understands that whoever is in the car has no need to leave it. There will be no impatient beep of the horn, no one standing on the pavement waiting by an open passenger door, no one coming into the café, blocking the light, a hand outstretched to the angel saying: 'Come away. Come away now.' There will be nothing but the car waiting, for as long as it takes. He understands that this is probably not the first time. Or the last.

The angel places her chair carefully back at the table, wipes a crumb from the surface with the blade of her hand. Looks around the café and nods. Then she kisses Rose on each cheek, goes over to Billy and does the same.

'Next time you come, my love, bring some of that homemade cider with you,' says Rose.

'Of course. It will happen. I believe it will happen,' says the angel.

Then she walks out, winged, to the brightness of the light, and the darkness of the car. Billy tries to see inside when she opens the door, but there is nothing. He wishes she would turn around one more time, but she doesn't. He remembers that they never asked her name.

The car reverses, pauses, then pulls away without fuss, moving down the street until it reaches the junction at the end where, with a distant guttural roar, it turns and disappears.

★

Suppose you were one of those Clifton flaneurs, or a faulty satnavver, or a bully-avoiding child, then you might have caught a glimpse inside the café after the car had gone. You might have seen Billy and Rose stood together at the window for a long, long time. You might have watched as Billy eventually returned to his seat and Rose cleared away the angel's cup and plate. You might have seen the low sun slanting into the café as if through a church window and decided, performing your three-point turn in the silent road, or hurrying on at the echo of your own footsteps, or back-tracking in your search for some edgy urban grit, that this was nothing more than the normal passage of time in some quiet corner of the city.

After all, what would you miss? Only that at 5pm sharp, Rose turns round the card on the door of the Headley Café from Open to Closed. And instead of waving Billy off down the street and then retiring upstairs to remove her shoes and massage her feet and feel the long, slow deflation of the day, she steps outside the door with him and locks the café up.

And rather than a stiff-legged stroll home, something warmed in a pan, a bit of telly and yearning for a life so distant he feels he cannot touch it any more, Billy walks with Rose, past the old butcher's window, past Klassy Kuts and the closed down corner shop, past the old bingo hall converted into flats, to a side road where the Malago emerges from its dank tunnels for a while to murmur alongside a footpath under a canopy of trees.

They pull at the stiff old iron gate to the path, wrenching it open enough to wriggle through, flakes of rust sticking to their clothes, rust on their palms, rust on their faces. There is an overgrown trail through a muddle and knot of brambles, saplings and nettles, until a broader pathway appears. They dab at nettle stings with spit-wet fingers then find a place to sit, easy together under a sky of deepening blue.

'Years ago,' says Billy, 'there was an old fella from Withywood, who swore blind that after soaking his feet in the Malago's water near this spot, he was able to rise from his sickbed and walk again.'

'Is that so,' says Rose. 'Fancy that.'

'Yep. Mind you, first time he went out for a walk he got run over by a bus…'

Rose laughs and shakes her head, then turns her face to the sun.

'She'll be alright,' says Rose, after a long while.

'I know. She knows where she's going, that one, even if it takes a good while to get there.'

Billy thinks about how much he has come to know of this

river, how the knowledge has accrued like silt within him. It has seen the Romans come and go, given its waters to Christian baptisms and pagan rituals alike. There have been celebrations and perambulations along its banks since the Middle Ages. And through that long span of time, the course of the river has been rerouted and slowed and pushed underground. And yet, Billy thinks, if you know where to go and when, you can find hazel catkins catching the light after spring rain, the red and yellow flash of moorhen beaks, flickering bullheads hidden under stones and tiny shoals of three-spined sticklebacks. There are places along the Malago where fists of the sweetest blackberries in the city hang over the water. And in the winter, whole fluffy plumes of Old Man's Beard hang on through cold snaps and bitter rain.

They sit for a while, Billy and Rose, listening to the water's passage and the birdsong and the city noises beyond, each thinking about tattered, shining wings and a passing angel. Together, just for a moment, they lift their eyes to what is beyond the rooftops and shadows, watching as birds lift from trees in the dusk.

A Public Performance

Magnus Mills

BY THE AUTUMN OF 1970 I was coming under intense pressure to buy a coat. A military greatcoat to be precise. Everyone I knew had one (everyone in the sixth form, that is) although they were officially banned from school. To avoid being left behind, I had to get one as well. There were lots to choose from. Barry, for example, had an ex-Army coat of olive green, while Mike's was blue-grey (RAF). Robert, meanwhile, favoured a huge brown over-coat that had been passed down through the Italian side of his family. It had a collar which could be turned up against the wind, and gave him the look of Giacomo Puccini in the famous photograph from 1910. The exception to the group was Phil, who always wore a US Army combat jacket. This was the other option open to me: I could either get a combat jacket or a greatcoat. The weather was turning chilly, so I decided on a coat. In that way I could both look cool and feel warm at the same time.

One quiet afternoon during half-term I caught a bus into Bristol and headed for a shop I'd noticed at the foot of Colston Hill. Looking back, I suppose the army surplus store in Gloucester Road would have been a more suitable destination. They had recently extended their range of stock to cater for the increasing demand, and no doubt could have readily supplied a garment to fit my requirements. The trouble was, I knew that everybody else had bought their coats there. I didn't want to wear the same 'uniform' as the rest of them, so I made my way to Colston Hill.

The shop I had in mind was called Visual History. It specialised in military artefacts, and its window was crammed with all sorts of muskets, blunderbusses and swords. Also, displayed on a mannequin, a very impressive coat. It was tailored from a fine grey cloth, and had two rows of gold buttons up the front. There were epaulettes of burnished gold on the shoulders, and gold flashes on the cuffs. I knew the moment I saw it that this was the coat for me. It clearly originated with the Russian Imperial Army, and I guessed it had once belonged to a Cossack. This was evident because the lower part of the coat was widely flared, an obvious prerequisite for riding a horse. Without a second thought I entered the shop.

There were no other customers, but the shopkeeper ignored me when I came in, and continued reading the newspaper that was spread out across his counter.

'Afternoon,' I said.

He peered up over the rim of his glasses.

'Could I have a look at that coat in the window, please?'

An expression of curiosity now crossed the shopkeeper's face. He glanced at me, then at the coat. Then back at me again.

'You're not wasting my time, are you?' he asked.

'No, no,' I replied. 'I'm thinking of buying it.'

The curious expression disappeared and was replaced with a sort of surprised half-smile, as if the shopkeeper was remembering some good news he'd heard earlier in the day. I watched as he climbed over a panel into the window display, returning a moment later with the coat. He quickly folded away his newspaper and laid the coat before me. It was very large and heavy.

'Pre-Revolutionary Russian,' I announced, examining the epaulettes in a knowing manner.

'Oh,' said the shopkeeper. 'Is it?'

'I think so, yes.'

After a long pause he nodded gravely. 'You know, I think you're probably right.'

'Can I try it on?'

'Of course you can. There's a changing cubicle over there.'

I entered a narrow booth and removed the raincoat I'd been going around in for the past two years. It was off-white in colour, and closely resembled the one worn by Steve McQueen in Bullitt. But I'd had enough of it. I hung it from the hook and proceeded to put on my greatcoat for the first time.

'Odd,' I said, talking through the walls of the cubicle. 'There don't appear to be any buttonholes.'

'No, there aren't,' came the shopkeeper's muffled voice. 'The buttons are only for show.'

'How do I fasten it up then?'

'There should be some little hooks inside the front of the coat,' he said. 'And some little eyes. You have to match them up.'

With some difficulty I did up the hooks. Then, to my delight, in one of the pockets I discovered a broad belt with a big silver buckle. This left no doubt that the coat must once have belonged to a Cossack. Moreover, it seemed to fit me perfectly. I adjusted the collar and emerged from the cubicle. The shopkeeper took one look at me and laughed out loud.

'Something wrong?' I asked.

'No, no!' he cried. 'It's fantastic.'

'Have you got a mirror?'

'Afraid not,' he said, wiping tears from his eyes. 'Sorry.'

The price was two pounds and ten shillings. At that time I earned one pound ten at my Saturday job, so the coat was by no means cheap. I decided, however, that it would be a good investment for my forthcoming winters as a student at some faraway university (or, as it turned out, polytechnic).

'I'll take it,' I said, producing a hard-earned five pound note.

The shopkeeper can't have had any other customers that day because his till was completely empty. Informing me that he would have to go and get some change, he left me inside the shop, still wearing the coat, and locked the door as he went out. Half a minute later he returned, accompanied by another man who I assumed came from a neighbouring shop. The two of them stood peering in at me for some moments before quickly turning away and moving out of sight again. When he returned for a second time the shopkeeper was smiling broadly.

'Here we are,' he said, letting himself in. He gave me my change and then asked if I'd like the coat wrapped.

'No, I think I'll wear it now,' I replied. 'Looks quite cold out there.'

'Suit yourself.'

He wrapped up my raincoat instead, and when I departed he insisted on shaking my hand. 'You've made my day,' he explained.

On the journey home a strange sense of solitude came over me. I sat on the bus in my newly acquired coat feeling quite aloof from my fellow passengers. Actually I felt sorry for them as they undertook their humdrum workaday journeys, while I enjoyed the unhurried timelessness of half-term. When we came to my stop I turned my collar to the wind and disembarked.

Of course, I was not at all surprised by my brother's response on seeing the coat. He was an immature fourteen-year-old and I took no notice when he asked me where I'd hired my tent. The reaction of my mother, on the other hand, was most disappointing. As I entered the house, she gave out a sort of gasp and instantly pushed a folded handkerchief to her mouth. I asked her what she thought of my coat but she was unable to answer.

'Want a cup of tea?' I enquired, reaching for the kettle. Without replying she rushed into the next room.

I was just stirring the pot when she returned. By now I'd taken the coat off and hung it up. After taking a deep breath, my mother asked me to put it on again, then she walked round and round me, looking me up and down. Finally, she undid the hooks and examined the label inside. It said:

MADE IN GREAT BRITAIN
XL DRY CLEAN ONLY
OTHELLO THEATRICAL SUPPLIES LTD

Kindly, my mother offered to remove the label.

★

The following Tuesday evening I went to see Pink Floyd at the Colston Hall in Bristol. They were touring with their latest offering, a semi-orchestral composition entitled 'Atom Heart Mother'. I had actually attended the first ever public performance of the piece earlier that summer during the Festival of Blues and Progressive Music at the Bath & West Showground, Shepton Mallet. Along with a quarter of a million others I'd endured two days of searing heat and dust. By the time Led Zeppelin played late on the Sunday afternoon there was virtually no drinking water available, and unscrupulous vendors were charging as much as five shillings for a can of Coca-Cola. As a callow youth I had believed this drink could quench my thirst and paid the fee not once, but twice. Ultimately, the event would be washed out by heavy rain, but not before Pink Floyd had made their long-awaited appearance late on the Saturday night. 'Atom Heart Mother' was an ambitious instrumental piece in which the band were augmented by a full brass section from a proper orchestra, along with a ten-member choir. There was also a massive TV screen showing close-ups of all the on-stage action, plus an extended light show and a firework display during the closing notes of the finale. Yet somehow I'd managed to sleep through the whole thing, having lain down on my groundsheet while I waited for it to begin. When I awoke it was the early hours of the morning, the showground was enveloped in mist, and all was quiet. Now, several months later, I had a chance to make up the deficit. Pink Floyd were on tour again! With my ticket in my pocket I set off for the Colston Hall. The first person I saw when I entered the crowded foyer was a girl from school called Alison who I was quite friendly with. (In fact, I quite fancied her and had asked her out a couple of times. She had declined the offer in a gentle, sympathetic sort of way, and we were now officially 'friends') She was standing with some people who'd left school the previous year, none of whom I knew very well. As I approached, wearing my belted Russian Imperial Army greatcoat, one of them looked at me, then said something to Alison and she glanced in my direction. Instantly, she put her hands over her face, closed her eyes and half-turned away. Sensing I was intruding on some private moment, I went and stood somewhere else. The first part of Pink Floyd's show included another new offering, an avant-garde composition entitled 'Alan's Psychedelic Breakfast'. This non-musical piece of work was to be found on their latest album, and the band had admitted in the music press that it was only a 'filler track' because they didn't have enough viable material. Nevertheless, a paying audience sat and watched as one of their roadies prepared his breakfast live on stage, accompanied by a 'sound-melange' of snap, crackle and pop, sizzling bacon, and, surreally, the voice of Jimmy Young. At the interval we filed out of the auditorium and into the bar for a drink. There was someone behind me giving the performance the benefit of his opinion, which was apparently at odds with that of his peers, who had roundly applauded it a few moments earlier. As a matter of fact, I thought he was quite courageous, announcing as he did that he thought the whole spectacle was quite absurd, ridiculous even, and a prime example of the folly of youth. To my surprise, none of his companions seemed to disagree. They smiled at me, one by one, as they passed me by. Turning up my collar, I went and stood by the doorway.

A View from the Observatory

Helen Dunmore

I'VE KEPT QUIET ABOUT it for a long time, partly because I thought Manjit might get into trouble over the keys, and partly for another reason. But I don't see how this story could bring her down. Her opening season as director at the Scaffold Theatre blew all the critics away. Everyone sees the glow around Manjit's name now, but it was always there, even when she was a skinny little girl. Things that I thought were solid, like school and home and growing up, were just shells to Manjit. She was the swan who'd got to hatch out of them. That's why Manjit got the job at the Observatory. It was all part of her hatching. There was a theatre-directing course that she knew she had to get on.

'It's the best. It's the only one, Zahz.'

Manjit always called me Zahz, right back from the first year at primary, and soon everybody else was calling me that, too. My name is ZsaZsa. My father just liked the sound of it, he said. I've sometimes thought that if my name had been Emily, Manjit might never have become my best friend.

So Manjit had to do this theatre-directing course. It was expensive, and you couldn't get funding for it. Manjit was back

69

home in Bristol, and she had two jobs, one waitressing in Browns, and the other working at the Observatory, selling tickets for the Camera Obscura and the Caves. I was working in a deli in Clifton, so I saw a lot of Manjit at lunchtimes, up at the Observatory. I'd been to uni, but I didn't know what to do next and I was back at home getting some money together, like Manjit. When people asked, I said I might go travelling. But I knew, and so did everybody else probably, that I wasn't the kind of person who goes off travelling on her own.

It was a hot September day. Really hot, really beautiful. Manjit and I sat on a bench overlooking the bridge, and ate the olives and smoked cheese and flatbread I'd brought from work. There were butterflies on the ripe blackberries that were just out of reach on the other side of the fence. We didn't climb over to pick them, because the drop is over two hundred feet, sheer to the Portway below. The sun glittered on the cars crossing the bridge.

'It's a great day for the Camera,' I said.

The Camera Obscura always worked best on a clear bright day. Manjit let me in free. I liked it when there was nobody else there; I liked the echo of my feet as I climbed the staircase that wound its way up the tower. If the door to the Camera chamber was open, that meant nobody was in there and I could take possession. Sometimes Manjit came up with me, and that was all right in a different way, because of the stories she told.

You go inside, you close the door and wait until your eyes get used to the dark. There in front of you is the wide bowl where the images fall. It's a circular screen, so big you have to edge your way around it sideways, pulling the wooden handle that alters the Camera's focus and changes the scene.

Everyone looks for the bridge first.

There it is, the bridge!

Look, you can see the cars going over the Suspension Bridge!

The Camera makes the bridge look even more fabulous than it does when you're walking across it. There it is in the bowl, slung over hundreds of feet of emptiness. The cars don't look important at all, but it's wonderful when a gull swoops under the bridge. Or even a falcon, sometimes. There's the mud, shining at low tide, and the river is as narrow as a worm.

If there are other people in the Camera chamber, you can't control the view. Somebody gets hold of the wooden handle and the bridge disappears. The view skims over the Cumberland basin, over the city houses and all the way around to the hills of Wales in the far distance. But when I'm on my own, I hardly move the handle at all. I watch the bridge.

I haven't looked into the bowl of the Camera for years. Even if I still lived in Bristol, I'm not sure I'd ever go there again.

When Manjit and I went into the Camera together, and she had hold of the wooden handle, she would watch the people and tell stories about them. If a dad was fumbling over his child's inline skates, Manjit would say, 'Look, Zahz, he doesn't know how to fix the skates. It's an access visit. His wife won't even let him in the house, she hates him so much. He's always here with his boy, skating up and down.'

There was a woman in a blue suit who stared out over the Gorge for a long time and then suddenly, secretively, brought something from a bag and flung it into the deep.

'Her husband's ashes,' said Manjit. 'He hated heights.'

'Maybe it was their favourite place,' I said, but already, the woman looked furtive to me.

We both liked to watch the trees. There's virgin forest on the other side of the Gorge. Right bang next to the city, land that's never been cleared, full of owls and murders and rare orchids. You look at the trees on the Camera and at first they're like a painted backdrop, then you realise that they're moving, swaying to the wind that's shut out from the Camera chamber. In real life I never notice how beautiful it is when trees move.

On that September day there wasn't enough time to visit the Camera. I had to get back to work. Manjit ate the last olive, and flicked the stone into the Gorge. We watched it tumble into nothing.

'I'm looking after the keys,' she said.

'What keys?'

'The keys to the Observatory. Just for this week, while Charlie's away. The keys to the only Camera Obscura in the whole country are in my bag,' said Manjit.

'It's not the only one, is it?'

'Pretty much.'

'You'd better look after them then. You're always losing stuff.'

'Don't you see what it means?'

'You get to lock up the Observatory at night, and unlock it in the morning.'

'Zahz. Keep up. Why just at night and in the morning? Why not at other times?'

'You're joking. You want to have a party there?'

'Not a party,' said Manjit with a flick of her hand.

'But listen, Zahz, it's full moon on Thursday. And the forecast's good. There'll be a big bright moon. Can you imagine the Camera by moonlight?'

'It won't look like anything,' I said quickly, even though I knew already that Manjit had planned it all and it was going to happen. 'There won't be enough light for the contrast.' Perhaps I was nervous about being on the Downs at night. When you grow up in Bristol you get it drummed into you that the Downs at night is not the place to be.

'How will we know unless we try?'

'What if we get caught?'

'We won't get caught. Anyway, I'm in charge of the keys. I'll say I was working overtime.'

Her face flared into laughter. I knew I wasn't being offered a choice.

Manjit borrowed her mum's car that night, the night, she had chosen for us to go. We parked near the Lord Mayor's House, which meant we had to walk up to the Observatory through the woods. Manjit was right, there was so much moon that we didn't need our torches. There were one or two people about, even though it was so late, but they weren't interested in us. I didn't like it, though. There were always strange sounds in the woods at night; I knew that. It didn't mean anything, it was just birds and animals and –

'What was that, Manjit?'

'Nothing. Ssh.'

We crept on, stepping as lightly as we could, along the path that skirts the Gorge and then rises to the Observatory.

'Manjit – '

'Ssh!'

Her fingers dug into my arm. We stood frozen, listening. A woman's cry echoed, cut off as if it had been pulled out of her throat.

'It's OK,' whispered Manjit, but her voice was thin. 'You know what this place is like after dark.'

The daytime face of the Downs was peeled away like a mask. The sunbathers and kite-flyers and joggers and ice-cream vans were gone, and something else was here.

'The keys, Manjit. Have you got the keys?'

I wanted to get out of the moonlight, out of plain sight. Manjit fumbled the keys and I kept watch. There were shadows all around us. As soon as I turned, they jumped closer.

'Manjit!'

The key clicked. We were in. Manjit pointed her torch

beam down, so no one would see our light. There was her chair, where she sat all day selling tickets. Manjit slipped past it, like the ghost of herself, and I followed.

I kept my hand on the wall as we climbed the stairs. It felt rough and safe. Manjit was up ahead, and darkness was behind us.

'You did lock the door again, didn't you?'

'Zahs, relax.'

The door to the Camera creaked open. Manjit's torch beam found the wooden handle. We closed the door and bent over the Camera's bowl.

I hadn't believed it could happen. You need bright sun for the Camera. But as we watched, the bridge swung into view.

'The lights are off,' I said.

'Maybe they switch them off after midnight.'

Even so, the bridge was darkly brilliant in the moonlight. The trees behind it swayed like seaweed.

'There aren't any cars,' said Manjit.

But there were people. A man and a woman. We could see them clearly now, coming over from the Leigh Woods side of the bridge.

'The fence has gone,' whispered Manjit.

'Which fence?'

'You know, the one that stops people from jumping.'

She was right. The high, in-curving fence was gone, and there was only the wooden handrail, chest high. The woman was hurrying, almost running, but the man was gaining on her.

'They've had a quarrel,' said Manjit. 'She told him it was over. He's desperate, he wants to make it up with her.'

The woman was really running now. She was more than two-thirds across the bridge. 'There's always someone in the toll booth,' said Manjit. 'She can go in there if she's upset.' But the booth was dark. There was only the woman, running, and the man close behind her. 'There,' said Manjit, 'he's caught up with her. I told you, it's a quarrel. They know each other. Look at them.'

He'd taken her in his arms, lifting her off her feet. They were one body now, vanishing into each other. They swayed awkwardly, dancing but not dancing, him holding her off the ground. The spread of overhanging trees hid them as they came to the piers, and we couldn't see them any more.

I let out my breath.

'I want to go home,' I said.

'No, we'll see them again in a minute. I can't believe how clear everything is in the moonlight. It's like a stage-set.'

A few seconds later a figure came out from the shadows. A man, walking slowly, almost strolling, you could say. Alone. Manjit and I stared into the bowl.

'Move the handle, Manjit. He's walking out of range. Follow him.'

But Manjit didn't touch the handle.

'It's not the same man,' she said.

'Of course it is.'

'Maybe she ran across the road, away from him. We wouldn't have seen her.'

I didn't answer. Moonlight lay in the bowl, washing the bridge into glory as it hung suspended over more than two hundred feet of nothing. Manjit's fingers dug into my wrist as we watched until the man had disappeared.

'Manjit – '

I heard Manjit's breath sigh out of her. She turned to me and her eyes shone.

I laid my hand on the screen and trees rippled over it. I could touch the trees, but they couldn't touch me. If I went out of the Camera chamber and opened the windows of the tower, I might hear something. Maybe footsteps, hurrying. Maybe a cry, suddenly cut off as if it had been pulled out of a woman's throat. But I didn't move.

We never talked about it, did we, Manjit? We never said another word about what we saw that night when the safety fence melted away, and the moonlit bridge printed itself on to the Camera's bowl.

Team Players

Valda Jackson

1987

I THINK IT WAS the way I told it that made them so vexed. I should have started at the beginning when Evelyn opened her door to me. Or maybe not there, on her doorstep in Hartcliffe, but at the basement in Bedminster where the damp was so odorous, I could feel the bacteria seeping into my lungs. Or no, not even there – I should have begun two doorsteps prior. Yes, I should have started in Ashton Gate: the stout, sleepy-eyed man, frozen in the doorway, listening to a woman's voice, sotto voce, behind him –

'Just Fuckin' Get Rid of Urrr.'

Obviously, I did not wait.

Over the telephone, all three voices had seemed friendly. I'd set out on the train from New Street at the crack of dawn and arrived at Temple Meads full of hope. But with that woman's voice still hissing in my ears, I was beginning to fear I would return to Birmingham without having found a room for the start of term.

I set off for the flat furthest away from the art college – Hartcliffe, my last resort – and flipped open my A-to-Z. I am mapping my route when I feel eyes on me. I look up and am surprised to lock eyes with a taxi driver, window down, one arm hooked behind the passenger seat.

'Where you going to, my lovurr?'

For a moment I say nothing. Perhaps he thinks I am someone else; someone he has been intimate with. Not without uncertainty, I read out the address in Hartcliffe.

'Oh, I knows where that is. I'm going that way. Hop in then.' He reaches across and the back door swings open.

'Gurt lush there, it is. 'Taint farr mind… You're not from Bristol then… where're you from? London? Oh, Birmingham's a big ole sprawler, innit? I wouldn't want to be driving about there all day… You a student, is it?'

I sit forward and survey his Roman profile, the heavy jawline; he lifts his chin, peeps enquiringly at me in the mirror, and swiftly looks away. I sense his discomfort on being caught. He wants my trust. He wants me to feel safe. I lean back in my seat, press my head against the head rest and let him hear my sigh.

'Oh, fine art is it – and where's that to? Bower Ashton I'll bet. Yes, I thought so. You'll love it there, mind. And I'll tell you what, if you likes animals, just you take yourself up that there hill – there's a lovely deer park. And you've got the cows across the road. It's gorgeous there. The lord mayor's horses are stabled up by the House. Oh there's a lovely sight for you. Took the wife and our Goddaughter up there just t'other day. We didn' half have some fun. Oh, she loves a horse, that girl – the Goddaughter. Six now she is. Horses, ponies, loves 'em. She's that age isn't she. Honestly, she'd have stayed all day given half the chance…'

I am falling into the warm, soft spiral of this man's voice; by the time he pulls up in front of the bungalow, my feathers are smoothed.

'Thank you.' I reach inside my bag. 'How much is that?'

'No. You put that away. I'm on my way home. Honestly now. You were just keeping me company. Good luck with the art, mind. And don't you forget to enjoy yourself now.'

★

I climb the sloping driveway to the bungalow. I give the door the gentlest tap, then spot the doorbell. My finger is poised to press; in the moment when I wonder whether it might appear impatient, the door opens. Though I am one step lower than she is, this tiny woman must still look up into my face. Her smile is broad and inviting.

'You're Vardurr, aren't you?' she purrs. 'Come on in my love. I expect you'd like some tea afore we starts.'

She flings wide the door and calls over her shoulder. 'Bo-ob, pop the kettle on now. Vardurr's here.'

I'm nearly two hours early. Neither Evelyn nor Bob mentions it, and I forget to.

'Make yourself useful,' Evelyn tells Bob as she hands him a plate of biscuits and nudges him towards the door. Bob hovers beside her as though waiting for further instructions. His wide frame makes his wife appear even smaller. Evelyn leans back and looks up into his face. Bob, dismissed, turns and walks towards the door. Evelyn, watching his retreat, calls out –

'And make sure to get the little table out, mind.'

I perch on a high stool at the countertop while Evelyn makes tea.

'I used to run the fish shop on the high street in Bishopsworth,' she tells me, '…and Bo-ob, he owned the butchers next door.'

'You had it covered then.'

Evelyn giggles, lowers her chin like a girl. I want to take her hand in mine, hold it for a while.

'We've never gone short. Of course, we're both retired

now. We sold up… ooh must be six years ago.'

We join Bob in the living room. Seated, Bob seems wider still than he did when standing.

'Sit yourself down, Vardurr.' Evelyn nods towards the armchair while she positions cups around the teapot. Bob picks up the television remote and turns off the volume. He still keeps an eye on the race though.

'Bo-ob, six years since we retired, is it?'

'No, dear. Ten.'

'It's never ten years, is it?'

'Ten years last July, dear.'

'Ohhh – It's ten years, Vardurr.' Evelyn passes me a cup. 'I've got a lovely fruitcake I baked yesterday. I 'spects you'd like some fruitcake 'stead of them biscuits.' And she is already up, disappearing through the door.

We drink tea, eat cake and Evelyn talks.

'We don't go very far these days now, do we, Bo-ob? Just to visit the grandchildren.' She turns to her husband. 'We don't go out much, do we, Bo-ob?'

Bob looks over at his wife and smiles.

'And even they're grown up now. We've got four grandchildren, Vardurr.' Evelyn takes a break to eat cake. 'Just one granddaughter though. I'd say she's your age, Vardurr. Isn't she, Bo-ob, Vardurr's age?'

Bob nods his head. Evelyn continues. 'When we goes to see them, we takes out the Jaguaarr.'

Bob perks up at this. 'Oh yes, the Jaguaarr. I gives it a polish…'

'We like to keep it nice, Vardurr. We keeps it off the road nowadays, don't we, Bo-ob?'

'Oh yes. I 'as to put it in the garage overnight. Tends to get scratches left out on the road.'

'Come on then.' Evelyn gets to her feet. 'Let's show you where you'll be.'

I follow her through the kitchen and out into the garden.

Although the self-contained flat adjoins their bungalow, it has its own entrance and the sliding patio doors of the living room overlook private green space where, in winter moonlight, a vixen and her family will romp in the snow, inches in front of me.

★

'Alright, my lovurr?' says the driver.

This 'lover' thing doesn't embarrass me anymore. With a warm 'thank you', I accept my change and find a seat. I rarely leave college this early, but today I rush to get the five o'clock bus from Bower Ashton to the centre.

There seems to be no difference between here and Bower Ashton, or even Hartcliffe. I had expected to see a few brown faces at least in the centre – on the streets, in shops, banks – yet each of these areas seem as white as the other. This only changes when I hit Stokes Croft and turn into City Road.

Raphaela has given me good directions, but I still use the A-to-Z. After a brisk walk, I arrive at the courts already warmed up. Raphaela – or Chilli, for Chilean – has set this up for me. Chilli is *The Student of Colour* in second year Fine Art. After weeks of eyeing one another at a distance, she and I finally closed in one afternoon in the refectory, and over cups of insipid coffee skipped formal politeness to dive straight into traumas past and present. Chilli has been living in St Paul's for over six years and though not a member herself, she knows everyone in the Team. I'm not great at netball – I'm not even a fan. But as *The Student of Colour* in first year Fine Art, I want to meet other black girls in Bristol. I hope to make friends here.

I enjoy the netball practice. In my school days, I was so disoriented that no ball game could be fun, but now I can catch, aim, throw, and feel not at all at sea. These girls, however, are fast. They're practised. But I think I do okay for a first timer.

The girls walk me to my bus stop in Broadmead. They do this even though they all live in or around St Paul's. It is dark now and someone asks, 'Anyway, why you livin' out there in Hartcliffe?' Before I can explain that I simply went down the list of addresses that I got from Student Services, another voice asks, 'Aren't you frightened they'll kill you?'

Well, I hadn't been afraid. Now, though, I'm not sure. But there is laughter, and I laugh along. It is in the ensuing quietness that Evelyn's voice pops into my head and I fill the silence with the story of how I walked into my landlady's kitchen one evening, and she had begun to tell me about a neighbour commenting on her renting her flat out to someone like me.

'But I takes people as I finds them – always have. And as I said to Bo-ob, so Vardurr's darrk. Well, she can't 'elp thaat, poor gurrl.' I pause at the audible guffaw, then continue in my landlady's voice, 'Why, underneath it all, she's as white as we arre.'

There are noises. 'Chuh' and 'Whaaat?' One voice rises above the others, bellows, 'And you never tump her!?'

Thump? Evelyn? I look about me as every face thunders outrage, shock. Scorn.

'Of course, I didn't thump her. Why would I?'

Eyes roll, cut away from me; there is one slow teeth-kissing 'Ste-e-u-ups' and 'What you expect from somebody who let teacher beat her in classroom?'

Ouch. I did not think Chilli would share that.

'I was seven –'

'Chuh – seven, six, five. No teacher nah gi me licks at any age.'

'Me neither.'

Their voices skip, twirl, and bounce around me now as their bodies did on the court.

'How you let white woman mess with your hair and you don't kick her arse?'

'It's why she livin in Hartcliffe, innit.'

'I can't imagine teacher getting weh with that in Bristol.'

'Black kids inna Birmingham mus' be saaft.'

Agreement. Laughter. I give up trying to defend what is deemed undefendable as the Team fall into unrelenting recollections of the posse in class, back in the day.

'...and teacher wouldn't dare lift finger on any one of us.'

'Remember that time when teacher calling out Maria Pinnock for some nonsense trivia?'

'And Maria never do nutten worth punishing, mind.'

'But Teacher sending her to Head Teacher office.'

'And one at a time all of us stand up ready to walk out – even some of the white kids did stan-up that day.'

'Innit.'

'Yes, you have to stand up to them, mind.'

'We had to train them.'

'Train dem good.'

'Let dem know seh they can't mess with us, innit.'

Raucous laughter.

I should stop them, tell them how when I get home late from college there is a fish dinner waiting for me. Or that Evelyn provides me with an electric blanket when I say I feel the cold. On Saturdays, she will stand on one side of my bed, with me on the other, and help me strip and remake it with crisp clean sheets. She refuses to have me go to the laundry or let me hand-wash my clothes. Nobody has ever done this for me.

At last, the number 76 pulls in. I step up and the Team recede, moving as one back the way they came, pumping shared memories into the air, leaping, catching, and dropping them into the nets of their familiarity. So tight.

I turn to the driver.

'Where to, my lovurr?'

The bus dips and climbs, darting its way towards south Bristol, filling with people and chatter. I want to get back home, slip quietly through the gate and into my little flat to be alone with my – what? This empty feeling.

I am alone on the bus by the time we arrive at Hartcliffe Way. The creak of the steel gate seems louder than ever. I shut it slowly behind me.

'Hello, Vardurr dear,' Evelyn beams out of her open kitchen window. Inwardly, I groan and pause in the glow of light.

'Never expected to see you back so early.'

Of course, her granddaughter came for tea today. I fix to my face a look of contentment.

'How is Niamh?' I say.

'Oh, she's busy as ever. Full of energy she is – just like you, Vardurr. But you are looking a bit drawn, dear... Let me unlock this door 'stead of shouting out the window. That's more like it. Come on in, Vardurr dear.'

Her look is as welcoming in the kitchen doorway as it had been that first day at her front door; but I also see excitement fizzing. This, I think, is the residue of spending time with Niamh.

'She's really enjoying the teacher training. It's hard work, mind. And I've been telling her about you drawing in the botanical gardens. She did some volunteering there back in the summer. Before she left today, she said again how she'd better meet you soon since you're all I talk about these days. But Vardurr, are you alright dear?'

And across the countertop, she reaches for my hand and holds it. I feel the papery delicacy of her skin, the tenderness as she tries to soothe.

'Did something happen?'

Evelyn's own eyes seem moist. I sense her fear for me.

'No... No, I'm really... really just... I'm really tired... and –'

I cannot keep the wobble out of my voice. Then, as if in competition for attention, there comes from my belly one bellow of a growl.

'Oh Vardurr, you must be starving, and me prattling 'stead of making you a cup of tea. I am an old fool.'

Now *I* hold on to *her* hand. 'No, Evelyn, it's not really your job to –'

'But it is my jo-ob if I wants it to be, Vardurr.'

Evelyn makes tea.

'I must meet her. Niamh.' I say this before I even realise how much I mean it.

'Oh, lovely, Vardurr? I told Niamh you were always so busy, I didn't think you'd have the time.'

'She's busy too. I'm around next weekend. Why don't you arrange it, then perhaps you can come to me, and I will make the tea.'

Evelyn uncovers a plate in front of me. Steam rises and I look down at the buttery haddock, new potatoes and peas. My belly sighs.

'Thank you, Evelyn.'

She shrugs, gives me that happy-girl look and waits while I take a mouthful. Then, with satisfaction –

'Yes, you can make the tea Vardurr, but let me bring the cake, dear, you don't want to be fussing with all that. I shall make a lovely fruitcake. I know you both love a good fruitcake.'

I swallow. 'Ok, you bring the cake, Evelyn. But now, since she's been hearing so much about me, you must tell me more about Niamh.'

The Water Bearer

Asmaa Jama

IT HAD BEEN THREE months since Ahmed disappeared. A makeshift shrine of dried flowers had been left in front of the Arnolfini where he was last seen, standing in a satin blue suit and matching durag. At first, his image percolated over local news channels, but after a month, his name was swallowed by a vague police report and everyone stopped looking. The world returned to normal. My brother Ahmed became just another missing 23-year-old.

After three months, two weeks and six days, we buried my brother. We gathered on a Saturday, at Arnos Vale Cemetery. I folded blue hydrangeas into the ground alongside an empty white cloth. The morning air hung around us. A few of Ahmed's classmates from his course at Central St Martin's were there, having made the journey up from London, along with the last of his friends from secondary school. Kids we had both gone to mosque with turned up at the end of the ceremony, looking shyly at the ground. I moved to greet them as the imam started the janazzah.

'May he cross safely,' he began, dipping in and out of melody. His voice streaked the air. A few people joined him, their vocal chords wet with emotion, bowing and pressing themselves to the earth around the grave.

Ahmed's only black professor, Mr Toussaint – a tall man with a mass of dark curly hair – stood at the back of the gathering, eyes closed and swaying. Later, he caught my gaze, and made his way over. He handed me some blue daisies, tied together with a black ribbon.

'Blue was his favourite colour,' he said.

'I know. Thank you. My father wanted to know if you want to come back for lunch.'

He nodded and the both of us walked towards the parking lot to stand by our battered Volvo. I watched my father embrace the mourners near the grave. He seemed stoic, standing as tall as he could manage, occasionally sitting down in the chair someone had bought him. My father's health had deteriorated this past season without Ahmed. I saw Nasra cross the cemetery towards him, dressed in a neon green dress, and help him out of his chair. The two of them made their way over to us.

Nasra was Ahmed's closest friend. They had met in secondary school, then gone to university together, Ahmed focusing on oils and portraits and Nasra on large iron sculptures, welded into fantastical shapes and painted lurid greens. In the last few months Nasra and I had got closer, drawn together in our shared grief; I would go to her studio at Spike and sketch in graphite, and she would spend the time mixing paints, searching for alien tones and shouting at intervals 'It's almost perfect!'

My father drove the four of us home without speaking. We took the route along the river, back to our house in Bedminster and pulled off our shoes. Mr Toussaint and Nasra sat quietly at the dinner table. I went into the kitchen and took the rice off the stove. My father joined me, looking for plates and cutlery. I handed them to him, and he wrapped me in a hug, smelling of pines and xawaash. We moved to the dining room with the butter chicken and bariis and sat down.

'It looks delicious, Adeer,' Nasra said.

'He was such a good student,' said Mr Toussaint, pulling at the chicken with his fork. 'So talented. He could manipulate the oils so well, the paintings always grabbed you – but he wasn't well at the end.'

Nasra shot him a look.

'You mean the blue series?' I asked.

Ahmed had been preparing for a solo exhibition in London; he was only in his second year and already gallerists had been circling him, his talent comet-like, endless and fiery. In those last few months over the summer, he was whittled thin by the long nights spent painting. Hundreds of renderings of a lone blue figure. He'd run out of space at home and was forever making trips back and forth to Nasra's studio, blue pigment streaking his arms.

Mr Toussaint looked down at his hands. 'If I had spotted it earlier, maybe I could have helped him. I thought it was normal, the obsession, the pace he was working at – I thought that was what he needed.' He twisted the silver signet ring on his left hand. 'He kept speaking about this figure that was visiting him.'

'Which figure?' I asked.

'I thought it was just part of the work –'

'Mr. Toussaint,' Nasra interrupted. She pierced him with a look.

My father stood up, switched the radio on and a qaraami song woozily filled the air.

'Your son is – was – brilliant,' said Mr Toussaint, changing track.

A tremble swept across my father's face. 'He needed to stop painting. It's painting that did this to him.' He turned the song up and sat in his rocking chair.

Mr Toussaint opened his mouth, then let it close. He saw his words were sliding off my father like water. 'Thank you for lunch,' he said, rising from his chair.

My father walked him to the doorway. After a while, I heard my father stumble through the kitchen and start on the dishes. Nasra and I got up quietly and went upstairs.

'He shouldn't be standing so long,' Nasra said, crashing onto my bed.

'He won't listen to me. This last week, the nerve along his back seized again, and he's been in so much pain.'

'Has he been using the arnica I gave him? My mother bought it back from Addis.' Nasra opened my laptop – with all the tabs left from my last browsing session. 'Zara, what are these?'

I grabbed the laptop from her. I had been looking for stories of other disappearances – the news was littered with countless young people in port cities disappearing, only to be found again, further inland.

'Nasra, he can't have just vanished. There has to be an explanation. Some of these stories of people being swallowed by water – it might be something supernatural.'

'Zara, I miss him, we all miss him. But searching for him in these places won't bring him back – I tried that.'

Nasra had spent the past three months putting up posters of Ahmed around the city, leaving threads on the internet asking for any trace of him. At one point Mr Toussaint had come up from London and organised a search party with her.

Her large afro framed her face and hung over her dark eyes. 'We have to let him go Zara, promise me you'll try.'

After Nasra left, I went downstairs, boiled a pan on the stove, and cracked into it cardamom pods, black tea bags and freshly sliced ginger. My father sat in the other room, the same song looped over, but this time my father's voice accompanied the singers, crooning softly.

'Wixii bada ku nool baa iga balangaaday inee biya isiiyaan.'
I joined him with two steaming cups of shaah. 'Do you know
what this means?'

'I understand some of it. Markaan beer cadaa – when my
liver bleaches white – wixii bada ku nool baa – the beings that
live in the sea – iiga balanagadeen inee biya ii siiyaan.' I
hazarded a guess. 'Promised to give me ... water?'

My father smiled, and the song ended in a static hiss.

'Who sang it?'

'I remember my grandfather singing this song. The sailors
used to sing it when they were lost and missed land. He used
to be a sailor too.'

My father went quiet, his face illegible.

'Do you want to go for a walk, Aabe?'

The evening was cool, the ground damp with rain. We
headed towards the harbour through Southville, stopping at a
church to rest, before continuing to Wapping Wharf. People
sat along the river's edge, finishing the last dregs of their coffee
as streetlights slowly came on. In this light, the cranes looked
skeletal and prehistoric, like they had seen too much. We came
to a stop as the tracks ran out: across the water, the Arnolfini.
Grey against the sky glinted the railings where Ahmed was last
seen.

'Zara, when are you going to go back to school?'

'I'm not missing anything important.'

'But you're in your last year – these exams mean you can
go to sixth form.'

I said nothing as I clung to the wharf's railings. The rusted
metal made grooves in my palms. I stared at the water lapping
the walls and saw something slip, silver, rise quickly and dip
again under the waves.

'Aabe, did you see that?'

He looked at the water; it was calm and smooth now,
reflecting the streetlights around us.

'I can't see anything. What do you want to do, Zara?'

'I want to be a marine biologist like Hooyo.'

My father inhaled sharply. 'Zara, I told you – you can be a marine biologist, but you're not training to dive.'

'What's the point of marine biology if I'm going to stay on dry land?'

'I said no.'

I looked out at the still dark water. My mother only came back to me in snatches, her voice trellising the air, her mouth held open with my name, the smell of fresh jasmine blooms.

'You remember her most, Aabe. Tell me about her.'

My father leant against the railings and ran a hand across his face.

'Please, Aabe.'

He fell silent for a while. Then:

'Your Hooyo was the bravest person I had ever met.'

I listened patiently as my father went back in time, retrieving the memories, slowly and surely, of their life together before Ahmed and I arrived. 'She had just finished university when we got married... moved over the water like she belonged to it... her father - your grandfather - was a seaman, did I tell you this?...'

A small smile warmed his face. 'You know, Zara, she tried to take me surfing one time?' He laughed. 'I was too afraid... so I watched her from the shore instead.'

As he spoke, I saw him, my father as he was, younger, face smoothed, still caught at the coast, his gaze fixed, to the horizon and her, liquid and ever-possible over the waves.

'You were only three and Ahmed five that day she went out for a swim in the bay...'

'Aabe?'

He gripped my hand tightly. 'Zara, that's why I don't want you going in the water.' He held me, frail as paper in my arms. 'I can't lose you too.'

We came home and made dinner. My father fried mackerel with chillies and garlic, the oil breaking over its glistening scales. I sat down at the table. Coltrane played softly underneath the sound of bubbling oil.

'Where did you learn to cook fish, Aabe?'

'Baidoa. When I was a boy, I lived by the sea. We went out in a little boat every day. I learnt how to weave nets, swim, catch and cook fish, and repair boats from my grandmother.'

'What are the beings in the water, in the song?'

'You mean ciddabadda?'

'Yes. They live in the sea, like a merman.'

'Merman?'

'Half person, half fish.'

'Something like that, but they weren't half human, half animal. They were something whole and different. My grandmother said she saw one once, with glowing skin-silver scales, almost like this mackerel.'

He peeled a scale off the cooking fish and held it up to the lamp. 'They say that once their body was like ours, that something happened to make them change.'

The pan hissed loudly as my father tipped in sliced tomatoes and balsamic vinegar. I plated the fish, took the pan off the fire, and we sat down to eat. The rain rapped against the skylight. While I took a bite of the mackerel, my father looked down at his plate.

'I remember, when I was leaving home, some people tried to cross over the water, in fishing boats. Some had cowries in their pockets and salt in their palms – I think they thought it would protect them.'

'Did you believe in their rituals, Aabe?'

'No,' he tailed off. 'Not anymore.'

He moved to the bookshelf behind us, his fingers flitting around the tomes, and stopped at a leather journal. He opened it and pulled out a water-stained photograph: him standing between two boys against a backdrop of ruined temples and colonnades, the light catching their smiles.

'This is me and my friends, Hashi and Mohamed. When I arrived in Cardiff I kept asking if anyone had seen them, or any of the people from Baidoa.'

'Did you ever see them again?'

He shook his head, his face cast in bronze, lost in the colonnades.

I waited for my father to fall asleep. Downstairs at the bookshelf, I pulled the worn journal out and returned upstairs.

Ahmed's room remained unchanged: bed roughly made, a pile of clothes in one corner, paints scattered in the other. I sat down on the bed. It still smelled like him – neroli shampoo and sea water. Hidden between the pillows, still, his scuba suit.

In the last month, Ahmed had started surfing again without Aabe knowing; he didn't like us wild swimming and had only recently come to terms with the fact that we went to Southville swimming pool, for years a chlorine-filled secret. I went over to the last painting Ahmed had been working on; it took up half the wall, the Indian ocean a mass of blue, and an oily body emerging from it, like a gutted fish, clotted. I flicked through the journal and found the lyrics to the fisher-song 'wixii bada ku nool baa'. I sang, remembering, and read.

It began two hundred years ago, the people who started turning into empty pools – scaled and silver things. The god of those waters was named biya-lag, meaning 'anything that swallowed'. Every year the people gathered everything they owned, gold trinkets, anklets, meat smoked on an open fire. The seas would gather clouds above them and the people would leave their offerings on the coast. If biya-lag accepted their offerings a single golden starfish would be left on the coast. It was always the youngest that found it overturned in the sand.

One year, a man named Samatar refused to make an offering.

His family had barely made it through the fishing season, with the fish too small to feed anyone. He needed the last of his gold to pay for the rice they would eat and so, after attending the ceremony, he slipped away, leaving nothing.

When it came time to fish, Samatar joined everyone else, in the small wooden boat left to him by his grandfather. Everyone returned but him. A week later, they found his boat overturned, adorned with a single white starfish.

The elders took this as an omen that biya-lag was angry and that it wanted flesh offerings to appease it. Boys were left on the coast – as a sacrifice. After a few months, people reported they had seen the boys amongst the living, Samatar among them. On moon-bright nights, they were seen walking out of the water, their bodies burnished.

At first, people dismissed these sightings, not believing anyone could return from the water, but soon the people grew more and more fearful – fishermen started returning to shore with broken nets, food spoiled, and water wells filled with saltwater. One night – no one knows how – the elders' aqal caught fire. Someone said they had seen glinting men at the corners of the village, watching the flames turn into embers.

The people stopped making their flesh sacrifices and left the possessions that the dead had once loved in life, hoping this would appease them, but each night another hut caught fire. Soon after, they decided to leave, taking their few belongings and migrating further inland.

A century later, the abandoned town Bay-doa was repopulated with new people moving in from smaller villages. When the war came, many tried to cross over the water and many disappeared. Some say the tides around that part of the country are the strongest. Others believe the ciddabadda are still looking for those that drowned them.

There was a drawing of a shadowy figure, and beneath it the words, *Samatar, the first ciddabadda*. They seemed to pulse slightly on the page. I shut the journal quickly.

I went back to the canvas. In the margins, Ahmed had scrawled '*safe crossing*'. I pressed my fingers into the raised marks. The charcoal came off but in the dark it was obsidian, gleaming.

The painting started dripping. Leaking. Moving inky and fast down my hands and arms. The ink reached my chest and ran down my legs, pooling cold around my feet. I shut my eyes tight. In for four. Out for four. I opened them to the ground, dry and warm beneath me.

'Zara?'
Ahmed.

★

Ahmed told her about his arrival. Before he was swallowed, he had seen it – the silver flash at the wharf that kept appearing in his dreams – and before he knew it, he found himself dripping into the ground. Arriving somewhere cold and dark, alone.

A single silver scale formed on the back of his hand. When he tried to peel it off, digging his fingers underneath in an attempt to loosen it, he realised he had to stop: it was embedded into his skin. Now his arms and neck were entirely covered, the scales migrating to his chest. Sometimes he heard the roar of waves but he never saw them, the landscape a vague muted blue; sometimes he saw Spike Island, its glass front lit like a lighthouse in a storm. When he heard a sound like tearing parchment split the sky, he had walked towards it, only for his breath to catch at the sight of his sister.

The two of them sat in silence.
'Do you know where we are, Ahmed?'
'I don't know, I've been here for weeks.'
'Months,' Zara corrected.

Ahmed pulled out the matches from his pocket. He had three left. (He had burned through the others so fast, hungry for a little sliver of light). He lit the match and for the first time, Zara could see his face. All of the contours of it were recognizable – but like it was recast in silver. When she looked closer, she could see the small overlapping scales that covered the entirety of it.

'Your eyes.'

They were wet and metallic. The match fizzled out. He moved away quickly but Zara reached into her pockets and pulled out the leather journal and handed it to him.

'I found this book Aabe kept,' she said, handing it to him, 'old stories, written in Somali. There's one story of a man who died at sea coming back with skin like hard jewels. Ahmed, you're changing into the ciddabadda.'

Ahmed flicked through the pages. 'Does anyone change back in this?'

A small amulet came loose from the centre, silver and engraved with a tiny cowrie and Arabic calligraphy swirling at the centre. Zara took it from him. It glowed brighter.

'I think this must be from Bay-doa too. Where Samatar, the first, was from.'

Ahmed paused on the last page. 'I tried to paint him.'

'Your blue series? I always thought that was you?'

'No, it was one of them. He kept appearing in my dreams, and the visions kept getting clearer and clearer. Zara, he was drowning.'

It was colder in the cave they sat in, like the temperature had dropped. Ahmed picked at his scales with his fingers.

'For months water kept finding me, in the bottom of my drawers, and my cupboards, in my shoes – always dark and bracken-filled. I kept emptying it out, but more would arrive. It was like this place was calling me.'

As Ahmed spoke, a whistling noise came from the air

above them. The walls of the cave shook. Zara and Ahmed scrambled towards the exit, where above them, the sky had darkened and pores were opening along its seam. The landscape was collapsing, shifting – glitching. For a moment, the harbour appeared with its tall copper cranes, the helm of the Matthew, before disappearing again into large slopes. Figures began to descend from the pores, whirring and pulsing with light. The sound of lapping waves was deafening. Zara shielded her ears while Ahmed stood by her, his own skin glowing in the presence of the other beings.

The figures landed and walked towards them. Their bodies glimmered. They were eighteen in total, covered in scales, with openings along their necks that resembled gills. Their eyes gleamed like steel. The rest of their faces weren't recognizably human – like their features had smoothed over time.

'I'm Samatar,' said one of them, his voice was gravelly and metallic. His scales had tarnished in places.

'He was the first,' one of the boys said, his voice clanging.

Ahmed turned to him 'You kept appearing in my dreams. What is this place?'

'We're inside of a prayer – something the first person who drowned uttered,' said Samatar.

Zara pressed her hands to her sides and peered at him.

'What did they pray for?' she asked.

'To live.'

'And are you alive?'

'Not quite. You see, no deity can bring something back from the dead. All we have here is more time.'

'But in the story, you came back.'

'And burnt them?' said Samatar, laughing.

So, the story was a lie. Zara looked at the people standing around her.

'Is it true the townspeople sacrificed them?'

Samatar gestured at them to sit; the others lay in various

positions on the ground. With his hands he pulled a small flame out of the air. For the first time, Zara could make out the undulations in the terrain: small dunes, of – now that she looked closely – fish scales. In this light, Samatar looked almost human.

'At first, I didn't think it was true that they were sending people into the ocean as sacrifices. I never believed in biya-lag. I just thought that the elders needed something for us to believe in. It's easier to rule people when they fear something.' He moved his palms above the fire and the flames leapt brighter. 'And we had nothing to give. Each year, we grew poorer and poorer. I saw people leave their inheritances on the shore, give away their family's jewels. And these weren't rich people. And what is a child, but a kind of wealth?'

'Is that why you're here too?' Ahmed asked.

'The truth is, I was the first. I was seventeen when they put me in a boat and sent me out into the storm. I didn't know that they would – that they could.'

Samatar stopped. He remembered the elders, the way they had been unflinching in their decision. They took his amulet, the one that let them enter the water and return safe. His mother had shouted out a prayer, but the wind snatched the syllables; it never reached him, or his rowboat, as he went out onto the waves, into the wide heart of the sea.

'Do *they* remember?' Zara asked.

'Only some of them. Most of them have forgotten by now. And it's easier that way. Forgetting. Sometimes, they wake up from nightmares crying for their parents. In this place, I look after them. They don't have to remember their parents are the ones that let the water swallow them. There is no god in these waters.'

The fire went out. The temperature dropped even further. Samatar and the others went to sleep; as they breathed, the scales shifted slightly beneath them. Zara shook her brother awake. She pulled at his hand and they walked a little way away from the sleeping bodies.

'I know how to get back,' she said hastily. 'Give me the book.' She flicked through the pages of the journal, scanning each page. There, scrawled in the margins, was the qaraami song in her father's handwriting and a symbol. Zara pulled out the amulet from her pocket. 'It's the same symbol.'

Samatar stirred. Ahmed flinched slightly. He regarded Zara warily, and took a step away from her, but Zara grabbed his hand.

'I need you to help me.'

'I don't know if I can go back.'

'What do you mean?'

'I was so exhausted all the time, Zara. I was drowning at school. When I got here, I slept for so long. This place – saved me.'

'It *took* you, Ahmed. It's changing you, making you forget. I know I can't ask you to come back for us. I know it doesn't work like that.' She felt the cold radiating from his arms. 'But I miss you, Ahmed. Aabe and Nasra, we've all missed you.'

A glimmer passed over his silver face. He scrunched his brow, looked down at their entwined hands.

'Sing with me.'

His body, heavy with the loneliness of the plane, leaned against her as she flipped through the book. She found the page with the circle symbol, and held the amulet as together they sang the words aloud.

'*Markaa beerka caadaa, wixii bada ku nool baa, balan iga gaaday, inee biya iisiiyaan.*'

The scales around them started glowing. They felt themselves lifted into the air, along with the sleeping ciddabadda. They kept rising until they reached the seam in the sky. Zara placed her hands over her head but a pore in the sky opened up, and with a bright snap, pulled them through.

★

Zara and Ahmed lay on the cobblestones that sloped towards
the river. Not far from them, the rowing boats sat stacked
against each other, narrow and ghostly like the ribs of a
forgotten creature. Waves lapped their feet.

Zara looked around: they were near Spike Island. She and
her father had walked this side of the river only hours before.
She reached for her brother and shook him.

'Ahmed?'

But Ahmed wouldn't stir. In the pale evening light, his
face was horrifying – half covered in scales, half greyed skin.

They weren't alone: around them, bobbing in the water,
the other boys began to stir. Samatar stood beside the boats,
mirage-quiet.

'Samatar,' cried Zara. 'He's so cold!'

'Water,' Ahmed murmured.

Zara looked at the scales: they seemed to be moving as he
breathed – each breath more laborious than the last. She
dragged Ahmed towards the water, his arms hanging lifelessly
over her shoulder. Before submerging herself, Zara put the
amulet around her neck, then submerged them both.
Underneath the water, Ahmed's scales brightened, and his
chest expanded. He opened his eyes and pulled them up to
the surface. Zara gasped for air.

Samatar was suddenly in the water with them. His eyes
were steelier, his scales raised along his back.

'It's hard being between worlds, isn't it?'

'You lied, you said there was no way to go back. The
stories of you returning were true.'

'Sometimes, you have to burn something down to start
anew.' The water rippled around him as his voice slipped from
him heavy and wet. 'Fire is cleansing. But I guess, you didn't

think to tell me that both of you were from there.'

Zara closed her hand around the amulet, and Ahmed clasped his hand over hers; the amulet glowed.

'Do you know what your father did, so you could be born here? What he did to his friends?'

Zara shook her head. 'No, they drowned. He said they drowned.'

'Or did he sacrifice them?'

Zara tried to imagine her father, his crestfallen face, capable of killing like that. She didn't know if that was something he could be.

'I'm telling the truth, Zara.' Each word of Samatar's sliced through the water like a blade. 'Those two boys, Hashi and Mohamed, they fell into the water and he wouldn't save them. He told them that biya-lag needed offerings – in exchange for safe crossing. Zara, he let them drown.'

Zara's blood turned cold as two of the boys swam over to them. Even after the erosion that seemed to happen with all their faces, she couldn't deny it was them: the boys in the photograph.

'He said he would come back,' Mohamed said, his voice wet as a well.

'He never did,' said Hashi, his voice like falling rain.

'Zara, Ahmed!'

They looked behind them and saw their father and Nasra waving at them from the promenade by the boats. Nasra ran down the cobblestones into the water, her moss-green dress mottling, and wrapping Ahmed in a hug. Zara's father followed – posters, of both of his children, falling out of his arms into the water. Zara swam up the cobblestones towards her father. He was frailer than before and looked at her with concern.

'He found you, didn't he?'

Samatar emerged from the river behind them, menacing

and silver.

Zara's father tried to pull her behind him. 'Zara, you must stay away from him.'

'Zaki,' Samatar taunted, inching closer, his voice a low whistle through the air. 'Tell her how you sacrificed them.'

Her father opened his mouth to speak, then looked at the swirling water around them, as if transported to the colonnades again. 'I tried to save them, Zara. He came to us and pulled them all into the water, wuu laqay. The only thing that stopped him taking me was the amulet my father gave me.'

'Zaki.' Out of the river, as one, rose Hashi and Mohamed.

Zara's father's knees buckled, submerging him in the river. 'But the water... it took you.' He splashed towards them, hands outstretched. He reached out and held their faces, cold and wet as stones.

'Hashi, Mohamed, hayati. I knew he turned you.' His voice was rough and breaking. 'I should have tried harder.'

The boys' faces, for a moment, glitched back to flesh. A smile broke across Hashi's. He put a palm against Zara's father's face and laughed.

'Is this what life has done to you?'

Zara's father smiled. 'I see you haven't changed. I never forgave myself.'

'Zaki, it wasn't your fault,' said Hashi. 'We remember now.'

Mohamed pointed at Samatar. 'It was his.'

The two boys circled Samatar. 'We remember what you did.'

Hashi made a chirping sound and the other ciddabadda emerged from the depths of the water, like a shoal of salmon, all at once and glittering.

'It ends here, Samatar. You can't keep us anymore.'

Samatar started towards them. 'Yes, I took you. I needed fresh bodies to keep that place alive. The elders didn't know bad-laq isn't a deity – it's that –' His face glitched, revealing skin warmed by youth. 'It's that place.'

He looked wearily at the horizon. 'I was angry for so long. I wanted everyone from the village to burn. But it wasn't enough. And it was easy with the younger ones. They believed me so readily when I came to them. They folded like fabric.'

With Hashi and Mohamed propping up each side of him, Zara's father waded slowly into the water, joining the shoal of glittering ciddabadda.

'You were a child, Samatar. The elders failed you. But if you keep this wound open, it will never heal.'

Samatar's young face turned to Zara's father.

'I want it to end,' he whispered. A small gasp of air escaped him, like a wound opening. His once large frame now looked like a child's. A left-behind boy.

Zara's father took handfuls of water and wiped it across both of Samatar's palms. He gestured for Nasra and Zara to do the same. Together they cupped the ciddabadda's hands for them and repeated the funeral rites, pouring water over silver palms. Zara's father spoke in an old language that sounded like a well opening in the ground.

For a moment, the boys were there, golden and almost alive in the sunset. And then, like salt, they were gone.

★

Ahmed stood in the centre of the room, at ease and smiling, as people milled around the gallery, pausing in front of his artwork. He watched Zara move through Spike like a bright comet, chattering excitedly in front of the canvases.

Large blue paintings of the ocean – of Samatar and Hashi and Mohamed – covered the gallery walls. The largest painting, on a wall all by itself, was a portrait of Zara, half covered in scales, her large dark eyes gleaming. *The Water Bearer.* He found Mr. Toussaint standing before it, quiet.

'There's so much blue, Ahmed. I feel like I'm under that water with you. What you've done with colour here. I can't quite breathe looking at this.'

Ahmed looked at him and nodded, both their eyes filling. They went and joined Nasra and Zara in the corner.

'How's uni?' Ahmed asked his sister.

Zara smiled. 'I'll be learning to dive soon.'

Ahmed squeezed her hand. Their father stood looking at the renderings of Hashi and Mohamed. They walked over to him.

'You captured them well.'

Zaki meant it; his friends from the other place, that many memoried place, seemed to smile at him gently through the pigment. He let out a breath, at last putting down the names he had been carrying, and looked back at this world – the one with both his children, the light hitting their warm faces, standing in front of him, flesh and whole. Entirely here. Entirely each other's. He turned back to the painting but the figures were now flat, contained in the portrait, their world fallen back under the water.

'I'm so proud of you, Ahmed. Thank you.'

Ahmed wiped tears from his father's face.

'Adaa madan, Aabe.'

Buckets of Blood

Tessa Hadley

THE COACH JOURNEY FROM Cambridge to Bristol took six hours. Hilary Culvert was wearing a new purple skirt, a drawstring crepe blouse and navy school cardigan, and over them her school mac, because it was the only coat she had. The year was 1972. In the toilets at Oxford bus station where they were allowed to get out, she had sprayed on some perfume and unplaited her hair. She worried that she smelled of home. She didn't know quite what home smelled like, as she still lived there and was used to it; but when her sister Sheila had come back from university for Christmas she had complained about it.

'You'd think with all these children,' Sheila had said, 'that at least the place would smell of something freshly nasty. Feet or sweat or babies or something. But it smells like old people. Mothballs and Germolene: who still uses mothballs apart from here?'

Hilary had been putting Germolene on her spots; this was the family orthodoxy. She put the little tube aside in horror. Sheila had looked so different, even after only one term away.

She had always been braver about putting on a public show than Hilary was: now she wore gypsy clothes, scrumpled silky skirts and patchwork tops with flashing pieces of mirror sewn in. Her red-brown hair was fluffed out in a mass. She had insisted on washing her hair almost every day, even though this wasn't easy in the vicarage: the old Ascot gas heater only dribbled out hot water, and there were all the younger children taking turns each night for baths. Their father had remonstrated with Sheila.

'There's no one here to admire you in your glory,' he said. 'You'll only frighten the local boys. Save your efforts until you return to the fleshpots.'

'I'm not doing it for anyone to admire,' said Sheila. 'I'm doing it for myself.'

He was a tall narrow man, features oversized for the fine bones of his face, eyes elusive behind thick-lensed glasses; he smiled as if he was squinting into a brash light. His children hadn't been brought up to flaunt doing things for themselves, although the truth was that in a family of nine a certain surreptitious selfishness was essential for survival.

Now Hilary in her half-term week was going to visit Sheila in the fleshpots, or at Bristol University, where she was reading Classics. A lady with permed blue-white hair in the seat next to her was knitting baby clothes in lemon-yellow nylon wool which squeaked on her needles; Hilary had to keep her head turned to stare out of the window because she suffered terribly from travel sickness. She wouldn't ever dream of reading on a coach, and even the flickering of the knitting needles could bring it on. The lady had tried to open up a conversation about her grandchildren and probably thought Hilary was rude and unfriendly. And that was true too, that was what the Culverts were like: crucified by their shyness and at the same time contemptuous of the world of ordinary people they couldn't talk to. Outside the window there was nothing to justify her fixed attention. The sky seemed never to have lifted higher, all day than a few feet above the ground; rolls of mist hung above the sodden grass like dirty wool. The signs of spring coming seemed suspended in a spasm of unforgiving frozen cold. It should have been a relief to leave the flatlands of East Anglia behind and cross into the hills and valleys of the west, but everywhere today seemed equally colourless. Hilary didn't care. Her anticipation burned up brightly enough by itself. Little flames of it licked up inside her. This was the first time she had been away from home alone. Sheila was ahead of her in their joint project: to get as far away from home as possible, and not to become anything like their mother.

At about the same time that Sheila and Hilary had confided to each other that they didn't any longer believe in God, they had also given up believing that the pattern of domestic life they had been brought up inside was the only one, or was even remotely desirable. Somewhere else people lived differently; didn't have to poke their feet into clammy hand-me-down wellingtons and sandals marked by size inside with felt-tip pen; didn't have to do their homework in bed with hot-water bottles because the storage heaters in the draughty vicarage gave out such paltry warmth. Other people didn't have to have locked money boxes for keeping safe anything precious, or have to sleep with the keys on string around their necks; sometimes anyway they came home from school to find those locks picked or smashed. (The children didn't tell on one another; that was their morality. But they hurt one another pretty badly, physically, in pursuit of justice. It was an honour code rather than anything resembling Christian empathy or charity.) Other people's mothers didn't stoop their heads down in the broken way that theirs did, hadn't given up on completed sentences or consecutive dialogue, didn't address elliptical ironical asides to their soup spoons as they ate.

Their mother sometimes looked less like a vicar's wife than a wild woman. She was as tall as their father but if the two of them were ever accidentally seen standing side by side it looked as if she had been in some terrible momentous fight for her life and he hadn't. Her grey-black hair stood out in a stiff ruff around her head; Sheila said she must cut it with the kitchen scissors in the dark. She had some kind of palsy so that her left eye drooped; there were bruise-coloured wrinkled shadows under her eyes and beside her hooked nose. Her huge deflated stomach and bosom were slapped like insults on to a girl's bony frame. She was fearless in the mornings about stalking round the house in her ancient baggy underwear, big pants and maternity bra, chasing the little ones to get them dressed: her older children fled at the sight of her. They must have all counted, without confessing it to one another: she was forty-nine, Patricia was four. At least there couldn't be any more pregnancies, so humiliating to their suffering adolescence.

As girls, Sheila and Hilary had to be especially careful to make their escape from home. Their older brother Andrew had got away, to do social policy at York and join the Young Socialists, which he told them was a Trotskyite entrist group. He was never coming back, they were sure of it. He hadn't come back this Christmas. But their sister Sylvia had married an RE teacher at the local secondary modern school who was active in their father's church and in the local youth clubs. Sylvia already had two babies, and Sheila and Hilary had heard her muttering things to herself. They remembered that she used to be a jolly sprightly girl even if they hadn't liked her much: competitive at beach rounders when they went on day trips to the coast, sentimentally devoted to the doomed stray dogs she tried to smuggle into their bedroom. Now, when they visited her rented flat in Haverhill, her twin-tub washing machine was always pulled out from the wall, filling the kitchen with urine-pungent steam. Sylvia would be standing uncommunicatively, heaving masses of boiling nappies with wooden tongs out of the washer into the spin tub, while the babies bawled in the battered wooden playpen that had been handed on from the vicarage.

In the coach, aware of her reflection in the window from time to time when the scenery was dun enough behind to make a mirror out of it, Hilary sat up very straight. She and Sheila had practised with one another, remembering never to lapse into the crumpled unawareness that smote their mother if ever for a moment she left off being busy. She was almost always busy. She had driven Hilary in to catch her coach that morning only because she had to go in to Cambridge anyway, to buy replacement school shorts and other uniforms from Eaden Lilley for the boys. The boys had larked around in the back seats of the ropy old Bedford van that was their family transport, kicking at each other's shins and dropping to wriggle on their bellies about the floor, so that their mother – who drove badly anyway, with grindings of the gears and sudden brakings – spent the whole journey deploring fruitlessly, and peering to try and locate them in the rear-view mirror. She had taken to wearing dark glasses when she went anywhere outside her home, to cover up the signs of her palsy. She stopped the van on Parker's Piece and had to get out to open the door on Hilary's side because the handle was broken. Hilary had a vivid idea of how her mother must appear to strangers: the sticking-up hair and dark glasses and the worn once-good coat she never had time to button up; her jerky burrowing movements, searching for money or lists in bags or under the van seats; her cut-glass enunciation, without eye contact, of bits of sentences that never became any whole message. When Hilary walked away with her suitcase to take her place in the little huddled crowd of waiting travellers she wouldn't look to see if any of them had been watching.

Bristol bus station was a roaring cavern: everything was greasy and filthy with oil, including the maimed pigeons. Green double-decker city buses reversed out of the bays and rumbled off, important with illumination, into the evening. A whole day's light had come and gone on the journey. Hilary looked excitedly for Sheila while she shuffled down the aisle on the coach. She wasn't worried that she couldn't see her right away. 'Whatever you do, don't go off anywhere,' Sheila had instructed her. 'Stay there till I come.'

Someone waited slouching against the metal railing while she queued for her suitcase, then stepped forward to confront her when she had it: a young man, short and soft-bodied, with lank light brown hair and a half-grown beard, wearing a pinstriped suit jacket over jeans. He also had bare feet, and black eye make-up.

'Are you Hilary?'

He spoke with a strong northern accent.

Hilary felt the disapproving attention of the blue-rinsed knitting lady, focused on his make-up and his feet. She disdained the disapproval, even though in the same instant she judged against the man with Culvert passionate finality. *What an unappealing little dwarf of a chap*, she thought, in her mother's voice. Of course her thought didn't show. To him she would look only like the sum of what she was outwardly: pale with bad skin, fatally provincial, frightened, with girls' school gushing manners.

'Yes.'

'Sheila couldn't be here. She's unwell. You have to come with me.'

He swung away without smiling or otherwise acknowledging her; he had only ever looked perfunctorily in her face, as if he was checking basics. She had to follow after him, out through the bus station back entrance into a twilit cobbled street and then up right beside a high grim wall that curved round to join a busier road. The tall buildings of a hospital with their lighted windows rose sobering and impassive against the evening sky, where the murky day in its expiring was suddenly brilliantly deep clear blue, studded already with one or two points of stars. The man walked ahead and Hilary followed, hurrying, struggling with her suitcase, three or four steps behind. The suitcase was an old leather one embossed with her grandfather's initials; he had taken it to ecumenical conferences in the thirties. Because the clasps were liable to spring open, she had fastened an elastic Brownie belt around it.

Unwell! Unwell was the word they had to use to the games mistress at school when they weren't having showers because they had a period. Hilary saved the joke up to amuse Sheila. Then she was flooded with doubt; why had she followed this rude man so obediently? She should have at least questioned him, asked him where Sheila was and what was wrong with her. Sheila had told her to wait, whatever happened, at the bus station. She opened her mouth to protest to him, to demand that he explain to her, and take a turn carrying the case. Then stubbornly she closed it again. She knew what a squeak would come out of it if she tried to attract his attention while she was struggling along like this. And if she put the case down and stopped she was afraid he'd go on without noticing she was no longer behind him, and then she would be truly lost in an unknown city, with nowhere to spend the night, and certainly not enough money to pay for anywhere. She could perhaps have hired a taxi to take her to Sheila's hall of residence, although she wasn't sure what that would cost either. She had never been in a taxi in her life, and would never have the courage to try and signal to one. And what if Sheila wasn't at the hall of residence?

Pridefully she marched on, though her breath was hurting

in her chest and her hand without its glove – they were somewhere in her shoulder bag but she couldn't stop to find them – was freezing into a claw on the case handle. Her arm felt as if it was being dragged from her shoulder. It wasn't clothes that made her case heavy, but some books Sheila had asked her to bring. Every forty paces – she began to count – she swapped her case and shoulder bag from hand to hand, and that gave a few moments of relief. She fixed her eyes on the back of the rumpled pinstriped jacket. Once or twice, on the zebra crossings, he looked back to check for her. Luckily his bare feet seemed to slow him down somewhat, probably because he had to keep an eye out for what he might be walking in. There were quite a few people on the streets, even though the shops were closed; sometimes he held back to let a crowd go by, perhaps because he was afraid of someone stepping on his toes. Perversely Hilary started slowing down too whenever this happened. She was damned now if she wanted to catch up with him. Even if he stopped to wait for her now, she thought that she would stop too and wait, as if the distance between them had become a fixed relationship, an invisible rigid frame of air connecting them and holding them apart in the same grip.

She thought she recognised the streets that they were walking through. When their father had driven Sheila over with her things at the start of the autumn term, Hilary had come with them; she had wanted to be able to picture where Sheila was when she wasn't at home. This shopping area was on a hill behind the city centre: it had seemed lively and fashionable, with tiny boutiques, cafés, a department store whose long glass windows were stuck with brown and yellow paper leaves. She had seen Sheila taking it all in from her front seat in the van, satisfied with her choice, impatient to be left alone to explore. At home they could only ever get lifts into Cambridge every so often, and anyway their shopping there was dogged by waiting parents, ready with ironic comments on whatever the girls chose to buy with their money. Dimly in the dusk now, Hilary could see the Victorian Gothic university tower where it ought to be, over to her right. Manor Hall residence where Sheila had a room should be somewhere off to the left, up past a little triangle of green grass. The pinstriped jacket struck off left, and Hilary was relieved. They must arrive soon, and she would be able to put her case down and be rid of her dreadful companion.

The road he took didn't lead up past any triangle of grass but downhill; it was wide, busy with fast through traffic but not with people. They left the shops behind and it seemed all at once to be completely night; the pavement ran alongside a daunting high wall to their left. The steep hills and old high walls of this city were suddenly sinister and not quaint, as if they hid dark prisons and corruptions in their folds. Hilary followed the pinstriped jacket in a grim, fixed despair. In spite of the cold she was sweating, and her chest was racked. She thought that catastrophe had overtaken her. She had made an appalling mistake when she meekly followed this man out of the bus station, like a trusting child, like an idiot. The only form of dignity left to her was not to falter, or make a worse fool of herself screaming and running, not to break the form of the rigid relationship in which they moved. She thought he might be taking her somewhere to kill her with a knife. She wouldn't say a word to save her life; she might swing at him with her grandfather's suitcase. Or she imagined drugs, which she didn't know anything about: perhaps drug addicts recruited new associates by bundling strangers into their den and injecting them with heroin. She didn't ever imagine rape or anything of that sort, because she thought that as a preliminary to that outrage there would have to be some trace of interest in her, some minimal sign of a response to her, however disgusted.

The pinstriped jacket crossed the road, darting between cars. Following, Hilary hardly cared if she was hit. He struck off up a narrow precipitous hill with tall toppling houses facing on to the pavement on either side. Because of the effort of climbing, she had her head down and almost walked into him when he stopped outside a front door. He pushed the door and it swung open. The house inside was dark.

'In here,' he said, and led the way.

Hilary followed.

In the hall he switched on a light: a bare bulb hung from the ceiling. The place was desolate: ancient wallpaper washed to colourlessness hung down in sheets from the walls. Even in her extremity, though, she could tell that this had been an elegant house once. City lights twinkled through a tall arched window. The stairs wound round and round a deep stairwell, up into blackness; the handrail was smooth polished wood. Everything smelled of a mineral decay. They climbed up two flights, their footsteps echoing because there was no stair carpet. He pushed another door.

'She's in there.'

Hilary didn't know what she expected to find.

Sheila was sitting with a concentrated face, rocking backwards and forwards on a double bed which was just a mattress on bare floorboards. She was wearing a long black t-shirt, her hair was scraped carelessly back and tied with a scarf. The room was lit by another bare bulb, not a ceiling pendant this time but a lamp-base without a shade, which cast leering shadows upwards. It was warm: an electric radiator painted mustard yellow was plugged in the same socket as the lamp. Hilary felt herself overheating at once, her face turning hot red, after her exertions in the cold outside.

'Thank God you've come, Hills,' Sheila said.

She sounded practical rather than emotional. That at least was reassuring.

Pinstripe stepped into the room behind Hilary. He put on a shifty uncomfortable smile, not quite looking straight at Sheila, focusing on the dark tangle of sheets and blankets that she seemed to have kicked to the bottom of the bed.

'D'you want anything? Tea?'

Sheila shook her head. 'I'm only throwing it up.'

'D'you want anything?'

Hilary couldn't believe he was actually talking to her. 'No, I'm fine, thanks,' she said.

'I'll be downstairs,' he said. 'If you need anything.'

They heard the sound of his footsteps retreating. Hilary put down her case: her hand for quite a few minutes wouldn't ease from its frozen curled position. 'Shuggs: what's going on?'

Sheila groaned: not in answer to the question, but a sound ripped from inside her, a low and embarrassing rumble as if she didn't care what anybody heard. She rocked fiercely.

'I'm miscarrying a pregnancy,' she said when the spasm seemed to have passed. 'It's a fine mess. Blood everywhere. Buckets of blood. You'll have to help get rid of everything.'

'I can't believe this,' Hilary said. She felt she was still somewhere inside the Bluebeard story she had been imagining on her way from the bus station. For a few pure moments she blazed with anger against Sheila. It wasn't fair, for Sheila to have spoiled her visit with this, her so looked-forward-to chance to get away. Sheila's mission had been clear and certain: to cut herself free of all the muffling dependencies of home and childhood. If she could succumb to anything so predictable as this melodrama – just what their parents would have warned against if only they hadn't been too agonised to find the words – what hope was there?

'What are you doing here?' she demanded. 'What is this place?'

'It's a squat,' said Sheila calmly. 'Neil's squat. I told them at Manor Hall that I was going away for a few days. They're not to ever know anything about this, obviously.'

'You'd be kicked out.'

'Uh-oh,' said Sheila, attentive to something inside her. Then she lunged from the bed to sit on something like a chamber pot in the crazy shadows on the far side of the room. Hilary tried not to hear anything. 'Oh, oh,' Sheila groaned, hugging her white legs, pressing her forehead to her knees.

'They wouldn't kick me out,' she said after a while. 'It's not that.'

'And who's Neil?'

'That's him, you idiot. You've just walked in with him.'

Hilary hadn't moved from where she stood when she first came in, or even made any move to unbutton her mac. She felt as if there was an unpassable waste of experience between her and her sister now, which couldn't be crossed. Sheila had joined the ranks of women submerged and knowing amid their biology. She realised with a new shock that Sheila must have had sexual intercourse, too, in order to be pregnant.

'I don't want Mum to know, that's why,' Sheila said. 'I'll simply kill you if you ever tell anyone at home.'

'I wouldn't,' said Hilary coldly.

'I just can't bear the idea of her thinking that this is the same thing, you know? The same stuff that's happened to her. Because it isn't.'

Hilary was silent. After a long while Sheila stood up stiffly from the chamber pot. She stuffed what looked like an old towel between her legs, and moving slowly, bent over as if she was very old, she lay down on the bed again, on her side this time, with her eyes closed.

'You could take it down to the lavatory for me. It's a flight and a half down, door on the right.'

Hilary didn't stir.

'Please, Hills. You could cover it with a newspaper or something.'

'Did you do this deliberately?' Hilary said. 'Is this an abortion?'

'No. It just happened. I might have done it deliberately, but I didn't need to. I'd only just realised that I was pregnant. I've only missed two periods, I think. I never keep track.'

'Who is the father of it?'

Sheila's eyes snapped open incredulously. 'Who do you think?' she said. 'I wouldn't have just sent any old person to get you.'

Hilary helped. Several times she carried the chamber pot down one and a half flights of stairs, holding the banister rail, watching her feet carefully in the gloom (there was only the one bulb in the hallway, which Neil had switched on when they first came in). She covered whatever was inside the pot with a piece of newspaper, then tipped it into the lavatory without looking and flushed the chain. Thankfully it had a good strong flush. She stood listening to voices downstairs, a long way off as if they came from underground, from a basement room perhaps: Neil's voice and others, male and female, subdued but nonetheless breaking out into laughter sometimes. Opening off the landing above the lavatory Hilary found a filthy bathroom, with a torn plastic curtain at the window, overgrown with black mould. An ancient rusted red-painted reel wound with canvas rope was secured to the wall beside the window, with instructions on how to lower it as an escape harness in case of fire. She ran the bath taps for a while, but although the pipes gave out bucking and bellowing noises and hiccupped bouts of tea-coloured cold water into the grit and dirt in the bottom of the bath, she couldn't get either tap to run hot.

'There's no hot water,' Sheila said. 'This is a squat: what did you think? Everyone goes into the halls to bathe. We're lucky to have electricity: one of the guys knew how to reconnect it. You could ask Neil for the electric kettle. What do you want hot water for anyway?'

'I thought you might like a wash. I thought I could put some things in to soak.'

'Don't worry about it. I'll wash in the morning. We can take all this stuff to the launderette later.'

Although they had always lived so close together in the forced intimacy of the vicarage, where there was only one lavatory and fractious queues for the bathroom in the mornings, the sisters had been prudish in keeping their bodily functions hidden from one another. This was partly in scalded reaction to their mother, who poked curiously in the babies' potties to find swallowed things, and delivered sanitary towels to the girls' room with abandoned openness, as if she didn't know that the boys saw. They had even always, since they stopped being little girls, undressed quickly with their backs turned, or underneath their nightdresses. It was a surprise how small the step seemed, once Hilary had taken it, over into this new bodily intimacy of shared secret trouble and mess. Sheila's pains, she began to understand, had a rhythm to them: first a strong pang, then a pause, then a sensation as if things were coming away inside her. After that she might get ten or fifteen-minutes' respite. When the pain was at its worst, Hilary rubbed her back, or Sheila gripped her hand and squeezed it, hard and painfully, crushing the bones together.

'Damn, damn, damn,' she swore in a sing-song moan while she rocked backwards and forwards; tears squeezed out of her shut eyes and ran down her cheeks.

'Are you sorry?' Hilary said, humbled.

'How could I possibly be sorry?' Sheila snapped. 'You think I want a baby?'

She said the pains had begun at three in the afternoon. She told Hilary at some point that if they were still going on in the morning, they would have to call an ambulance and get her into hospital: she explained in a practical voice that women could haemorrhage and die if these things went wrong. By ten o'clock, though, the worst seemed to be over. There hadn't been any bad pains for over an hour, the bleeding was almost like a normal period. When Neil came upstairs Sheila wanted a cup of tea and a hot-water bottle.

'You'll have to take Hilary out,' she told him, 'and buy her something to eat.'

Hilary had eaten some sandwiches on the coach at lunchtime. She hadn't had anything since then; she didn't feel hungry but she felt light-headed and her hands were shaking.

'I'm fine,' she said hastily. 'I don't want anything.'

'Don't be so silly. Buy her some fish and chips or something.'

Hilary was too tired not to be obedient. She put on her mac and followed Neil downstairs, as if their fatal passage round the city had to recommence. At least this time she wouldn't be carrying her case. She waited on the street outside; he said he had to fetch the others.

'By the way,' he added, not looking at her, 'I shouldn't mention anything. They just think Sheila's got a tummy bug. They'd be upset.'

'OK,' Hilary mumbled. Furiously she thought to herself that she wouldn't have spoken to his friends about her sister if he had tortured her. *You silly little man*: she imagined herself saying. *How dare you think I care about upsetting them?* She tipped back her head and looked up the precipitous fronts of the houses to the far-off sky, studded with cold stars.

She noticed that Neil had put on shoes to come out this time; a pair of gym shoes, gaping without laces. His friend Julian had jug ears and long dyed blond hair; Gus was shy and lumpish, like a boy swelled to man-size without his face or body actually changing to look grown-up. Becky was a pretty girl in a duffel coat, who giggled and swivelled her gaze too eagerly from face to face: she couldn't get enough of her treat, being the only girl and having the attention of three men. She knew instinctively that Hilary didn't count. Even her patronising was perfunctory: she reminisced about her own A levels as if she was reaching back into a long-ago past.

'You've chosen all the easy ones, you clever thing! My school forced me to do double maths, it was ghastly.'

'Are you sure you're not hungry?' Neil said to Hilary as they hurried past a busy chip shop with a queue. 'Only if we don't stop we're in time for the pub. You could have some crisps there.'

Hilary gazed into the bright steamy window, assaulted by the smell of the chips, weak with longing. 'Quite sure,' she said. She had never been into a pub in her life. There was a place in Haverhill where some of the girls went from school, but she and Sheila had always despised the silly self-importance of teenage transgression. It was impossible to imagine ever wanting to enter the ugly square red-brick pub in the village, where the farm labourers drank, and the men from the estate who worked in the meat-packing factory. Neil's pub was a tiny cosy den, fumey light glinting off the rows of glasses and bottles. The stale breath of it made Hilary's head swim; they squeezed into red plush seats around a table. Neil didn't ask her what she wanted, but brought her a small mug of brown beer and a packet of crisps and one of peanuts. She didn't like the taste of the beer but because the food was so salty she drank it in thirsty mouthfuls, and then was seized by a sensation as if she floated up to hang some little way above her present situation, graciously indifferent, so that her first experience of drunkenness was a blessed one.

When the pub closed they came back to the house and sat around a table in the basement kitchen by candlelight: the kitchen walls were painted crudely with huge mushrooms and blades of grass and giant insects, making Hilary feel as if she was a miniature human at the deep bottom of a forest. She drank the weak tea they put in front of her. The others talked about work and exams. Becky was doing biological sciences, Gus was doing history, Julian and Neil seemed to be doing English. Hilary couldn't believe that they sounded just like girls at school, scurrying in the rat-run of learning and testing, trying to outdo one another in protestations of how little work they'd done. Not once did any of them actually speak seriously about their subjects. Hilary felt so deeply disappointed in university life that on the spot she made up her mind to dedicate herself to something different and nobler, although she wasn't clear what. Neil and Julian were concentrating upon sticking a brown lump of something on a pin and roasting it with a match. From her indifferent distance she supposed this must be drugs, but she wasn't frightened of that now.

'Don't tell your daddy the vicar what you've seen,' said Neil.

She was confused – did the others know what had happened after all? – until she realised that he meant the brown lump.

'Are you two really from a vicarage?' asked Becky. 'It's like something out of a book.'

'We can't offer the respectability that Hilary's used to,' Neil said. 'She'll have to slum it here for a few days.'

Hilary could see that Neil was the centre of all the others' attention. At least he had not joined in when the others were fluttering and fussing about their work; he had smiled to himself, licking the edges of little pieces of white paper and sticking them together as if none of it bothered him. He had an air as if he saw through the sham of it all, as if he came from a place where the university didn't count for much: she could see how this had power over the others. He didn't say much but when he spoke it was with a deliberate debunking roughness that made the others abject, ashamed even of the feel in their mouths of their own nice eager voices.

Becky told Neil flirtatiously that he would have to be on his best behaviour, while Hilary was staying. 'No swearing,' she said. 'Cause I can see she's a nice girl.'

'Fuck,' he said. 'I hadn't thought of that. Fuck that.'

Hilary thought of the farm boys at home, who called sexual words when she and Sheila had to walk past them in their school uniform. She had always thought, however much it tortured her, that they had an obscure right to do it because of their work. In the winter mornings from the school bus you could see the frozen mists rising up out of the flat colourless fields, and figures bent double with sacks across their shoulders, picking Brussels sprouts, or sugar beeting. But Neil was here, wasn't he, at university? He'd crossed over to their side, the lucky side. Whatever she thought of her life, she knew it was on the lucky side, so long as she wasn't picking Brussels sprouts or meat-packing.

No one had said anything since she arrived about where Hilary was to sleep. Sheila was supposed to have booked a guest room for her at Manor Hall, but of course she couldn't go there now. When she couldn't hold herself upright at the kitchen table any longer she climbed upstairs to ask what she should do, but Sheila was asleep, breathing evenly and deeply. Her forehead was cool. Hilary kept all her clothes on and wrapped herself in an old quilt that Sheila had kicked off; she curled up to sleep on the floor beside the bed. At some point in the night she woke, frozen rigid and harrowed by a bitter draught blowing up through the bare floorboards; she climbed into the bed beside Sheila who snorted and heaved over.

Under the duvet and all the blankets it smelled of sweat and blood, but it was warm. When she woke again it was morning and the sun was shining.

'Look at the patterns,' Sheila said.

She was propped up calmly on one elbow on the pillow and seemed returned into her usual careful self-possession. Hilary noticed for the first time that the room was painted yellow; the sun struck through the tall uncurtained windows and projected swimming squares of light onto the walls, dancing with the movements of the twiggy tops of trees which must be growing in a garden outside.

'Are you all right?' she asked.

Sheila ignored the question as if there had never been anything wrong.

'How did you get on with everybody last night?'

'We went to a pub.'

'Oh, which one?' She interrogated Hilary until she was satisfied that it must have been the Beaufort. 'We often go there,' she said enthusiastically. 'It's got a great atmosphere, it's really local.'

'When I told them we lived in a vicarage,' Hilary said, 'one of them asked if we were Catholics.'

'That's so funny. I bet I know who that was. What did you think of Neil?'

Hilary was cautious. 'Is he from the north?'

'Birmingham, you idiot. Couldn't you tell? Such a pure Brummie accent.'

'He wasn't awfully friendly.'

Sheila smiled secretively. 'He doesn't do that sort of small talk. His dad works as a tool setter at Lucas's, the engineering company. No one in his family has been to university before. His parents don't have money, compared to most of the students here. He gets pretty impatient with people, you know, who just take their privilege for granted.'

Hilary felt like a child beside her sister. What had happened yesterday marked Sheila as initiated into the adult world, apart from her, as clearly as if she was signed with blood on her forehead. She supposed it must be the unknown of sexual intercourse which could transform things in this way that children couldn't see: Neil's self-importance into power, for instance. At the same time as she was in awe of her sister's difference, Hilary also felt a stubborn virgin pride. She didn't want ever to be undone out of her scepticism, or seduced into grown-up credulous susceptibility.

'But doesn't he think that we're poor, too?' she asked fiercely. 'Have you told him? Does he have any idea?'

'It's different,' said Sheila with finality. 'It's just different.'

When Hilary drove in the summer with her father in the Bedford van, to pick up Sheila and all her things at the end of her first year, she was waiting for them of course at Manor Hall, as if there had never been any other place, any squat whose kitchen was painted with giant mushrooms. Hilary understood that she was not ever to mention what had happened there, not even when she and Sheila were alone. Because they never wore the memory out by speaking of it, the place persisted vividly in her imagination.

She had stayed on in that house for almost a week: she had arrived on Monday and her return ticket was for Saturday. Sheila rested for the first couple of days, sleeping a lot, and Hilary went out on her own, exploring, going round the shops. On Sheila's instructions she took several carrier bags of bloody sheets and towels to the launderette, where she sat reading Virginia Woolf while the washing boiled. There seemed to be a lot of hours to pass, because she didn't want to spend too much time in Sheila's room; she shrank from the possibility of getting in the way between Sheila and Neil. A couple of times she went to the cinema in the afternoon by herself. They all went out to pubs every evening and she got used to drinking beer, although she didn't get to like it. While the others joked and drank and smoked, she sat in a silence that must have looked gawky and immature, so that she was sure Sheila despaired of her, although Sheila must also surely have known that she found the conversation impossible to join because it was so tepid and disappointing, gossip mostly about people she'd never met. Sheila, who had been aloof and not popular at school, seemed to be working hard to make these people like her. She made herself brighter and funnier and smaller than her real self, Hilary thought. She surrounded Neil in particular with such efforts of admiration, prompting him and encouraging him and attributing ideas to him, while he smiled in lazy amusement, rolling up his eternal cigarettes. At least they weren't all over each other, they didn't cling together in public. Hilary even feared for Neil, thinking that he shouldn't trust her sister, he should wonder what dark undertow might follow after such a glittering bright flood.

By the end of the week Sheila was well enough to go to lectures again, and on the Saturday she came to the bus station to see Hilary off. She insisted on carrying Hilary's suitcase, which swung in her hand as light as if there was nothing in it now that their father's old dictionaries of classical mythology had been unloaded.

'I didn't feel anything, you know,' Sheila said as they walked, as if she was picking up on some discussion they had only broken off a few moments before, although in fact they hadn't talked once, since it was over, about what had happened to her. 'I mean, apart from physically. Just like a tummy upset. That's all it was: a nuisance.'

'All right, if you say so.'

For the first time Sheila talked about her studies. She had to write an essay on the Oresteia which she said was all about the sex war, female avenging Furies and male reason.

'*The gods are disgusted at you,*' she said gleefully. 'Apollo to the Furies. *Apoptustoi theosis. Never let your filth touch anything in my sacred shrine.*'

When Hilary was in her seat in the coach, Sheila stayed hanging around outside the window although Hilary signed to her to go, there was no need to wait. They laughed at one another through the glass, helpless to communicate: for the first time they were in tune together as they used to be. Sheila mouthed something and Hilary mimed elaborately: frowned, shook her head, shrugged her shoulders. She couldn't understand. Sheila put her face close to the glass and cupped her hands round her mouth, shouting. She was wearing a woollen knitted hat with knitted flowers pulled down over her ears.

'Give my love to everybody!'

Hilary saw that all of a sudden her sister didn't want her to go. She was seized then by an impulse to struggle off the coach, to stay and fight, as if Sheila had after all been abducted by a Bluebeard: she felt focused as a crusader in her opposition to Neil. She even half turned round in her seat, as if to get out. But there was a man in the seat beside her, she would have had to ask him to move, he was settled behind his newspaper. The moment and the possibility passed. The coach reversed, the sisters waved frantically, and then Sheila was gone and Hilary subsided into her solitude, keeping her face averted from the man who had seen too much of her excitement, and whose newspaper anyway would make her sick if she accidentally read any of the headlines.

Above the city buildings the sky was blue and pale with light, drawn across by thin skeins of transparent cloud. Beyond the outskirts of the city everything was bursting with the spring growth which was further on over here than in the east. The tips of the hedgerows and the trees, if they hadn't yet come into leaf, gave off a red haze where the twigs swelled and shone. It seemed extraordinary to Hilary that her life must at some point soon change as completely and abruptly as Sheila's had, so that everything familiar would be left behind. She sat with bubbles of excitement rising in her chest. The scruffy undistinguished countryside outside the coach window seemed to her beautiful. It desolated her to think that when she was dead she wouldn't be able to see it: cows, green hummocky fields, suburban cottages of weathered brick, a country factory with smashed windows, an excited spatter of birds thrown up from a tree. Then she started to see these things as if she was dead already, and they were persisting after her, and she had been allowed back, and must take in everything hungrily while she had the chance, every least tiny detail.

The Cycle

Shagufta K. Iqbal

Dedicated to Sofia, Yaz, and Samira

FAREEDA FINDS HERSELF once again standing in a garden with
a green bicycle at her side. The sun is beating down and,
according to her phone, this is the perfect weather for a ride.
The last time she cycled, she was twelve. Beautifully green,
with a white seat and handlebars – it even came with a little
bell, a fairy magic DING, DING! At the age of five she'd
begged her father for a bike, and seven years later she finally
got one. Not long after he bought her the cycle, her father left.
Walked out as though he needed fresh air. The tune of the
Teletubbies chimed in the background, an absurd layer to the
adult shouting, and then there was the blurry outline of her
father through the glass panels of their front door, his walk
fixed and resolute, as though he had somewhere he urgently
needed to be. Now, nearly three decades on, Fareeda stands
with her hand placed on the saddle of a ladies Boardman, a
shade of green reminiscent of her childhood bike. It is a good
25 minutes to the cycle path, and she holds the cycle by the
handles as if it were a runaway bull.

After her father left, her mother had turned away from the
door and looked at Fareeda. 'Sweet French toast?' she chirped,
waltzing into the kitchen, pinning her dark curly hair above

her head. She was a tiny woman, all curves and eyes, hair like a raven, and a bright freckled face. She pulled her purple cardi close to herself. Her shoulder pads drowned her slight neck. This was how her mother dealt with pain: a reorganising of herself, and then a frenzy of pulling ingredients out of their cupboards to make pancakes, puff pastries, tarts, jams. The kitchen windows would steam with boiling, frying, sizzling and baking.

Fareeda and her sister were put to bed earlier than usual. The act tired their mother; she needed privacy for her grief. At 7pm, with the girls in their beds, the whole house shook with sadness.

Fareeda returns to the old streets. They bring back memories she has tried so hard to bury. The city has changed and contorted, consumed pockets of history, regurgitated new spaces in their stead, and yet it is as familiar as ever. Despite the new buildings and its façade as a contemporary major city, the place still holds many of its insecurities; a big town with city dreams, unable to confront its past, unable to live up to its reputation as a free spirit. She almost laughs at being back here, how similar she is to this place. The city's identity swings on a pendulum: at one end it is still the remnants of a slave-trading port city, and at the other, it tries so hard to convince the world that it is an environmentally-friendly arts hub; a city of festivals and hot air balloons. No matter how hard she tries to escape, her feet always land firmly back here whenever calamity strikes. And Fareeda is good at turning small events into life-changing disasters.

She turns onto St Mark's Road to meet Rooqia for a coffee and a catch up before they meet the Muslim women's cycle club. She makes a mental note to purchase some vegetarian samosas from Jeevan's – the best Bristol has to offer – on her way back home. Fareeda looks at her watch, a Casio throwback, and realises she is unusually early. She walks up the road, her cycle at her side, and passes the long-standing grocery store. She notices new bakeries and new stores, offering gluten free and vegan goods, and wonders how long the halal butchers will be able to stay. She recalls a Facebook post about making St Mark's Road more pedestrian-friendly by reducing car access. After reading a few comments, she'd closed the app. Everything seemed so black and white. There is no room for nuance these days. Once, she would have taken a strong political stance, vehemently defended areas against gentrification and signed endless petitions. But these days she is tired, and has lost her love for this stubborn place, so in denial of itself. She stops outside Thali Café, locks her cycle – green and unused – and enters the café through its bright pink doors. She sends a text to Rooqia.

Ordered you a chai, want something sweet with it?

Back outside, Fareeda takes a seat at the table on the street, under the window of the shop. She watches her cycle and waits for her order to arrive. Reties her shoelaces. Flicks through her phone. Anxious to be on her own.

Rooqia messages back, ignoring her question.

Be there in 10!

Fareeda looks at the cycle. It's only been with her for two weeks and Rooqia has insisted they spend all summer cycling the Bristol to Bath cycle path. She'd recalled Fareeda's half-hearted attempt at learning to ride when they were young.

'You didn't even make it out your garden – that poor bike!'

Fareeda recalls that summer differently. Poor bike? She had been surprised at the effort it took to stay upright on the cycle. In her small back garden, she had tried to balance herself against the pebbledash wall, the green cycle heavy and unsteady beneath her, its white seat uncomfortable. Her mother was in the kitchen, hands full of soap suds, shouting encouragement from the kitchen window. Her soapy hands directed that Fareeda let go of the wall and trust her own body. Fareeda's five-year-old sister, in a pink frill dress and two ponytails in ribbons, watched with boredom. She realised Fareeda was not going to let go of the wall, and walked away, bubble wand in hand. Fareeda still remembers her sister's small face, eyebrows furrowed in the heat of early August, her arms flailing trying to pop all the bubbles descending around her. Eventually, Fareeda managed to let go. She shook forward a few metres, only to graze her arm and knee against the wall, unable to stop the cycle. By the time she was twelve, she decided it was too late. She was too old to conquer the unforgiving hills of Bristol. The cycle was left in the garden against the wall and began to rust next to the coriander, mint and tomato pots her mother planted and let die.

When Fareeda became a teenager, she felt she had dreamed up a man called Father. Most of the time she could convince herself that it had always been the three of them. Then she would see the green Raleigh cycle in the garden, and suddenly her breath would leave her. In later years, she would see him sometimes: driving past her school, walking into a shop. Brief moments of recognising a part of yourself only to lose it in a crowd, across a busy street, watching it disappear inside a dilapidated shopping centre.

Her own cycle abandoned in the garden, Fareeda watched the boys cycle to and from school with an easy confidence. They would ride up and down the streets on shiny new bikes, coveted BMXs. They could be seen following the small stretch of backstreets that ran along the slight body of the River Frome, shadowed by the M32 motorway. Here, the boys would show off to one another their new tricks and skills. A one-wheel ride down the road, front handlebars lifted up. Or hopping from front wheel to back wheel, sometimes down a series of stairs. To Fareeda, it seemed as though the bike was an extension of their limbs. Everything gliding without the need to think. They looked adventurous and free; the city stretched out before them.

'If you complain too much, there is a little beer garden along the way which we can stop at. They do the best homemade lemonade. But trust me, it'll be fun. You'll enjoy it.'

Rooqia has a constant steady will. She is never one to give up. Nor is she one to over-dream, seeming to get through life in a series of straightforward milestones. Fareeda spent most of her days in Rooqia's family home when they were children. Everything about their home was what Fareeda had dreamed of. Rooqia's parents, with their slow, quiet lives. She would watch the friendship that existed between them and wish it for her own life. Her mother, who seemed grateful at the environment young Fareeda had found herself in, was at other times bitter, struggling with her own sense of inadequacy, loneliness, and exclusion from her daughter's life.

'I cannot be everything at once. One day you will understand.'

Fareeda's mother would say this to her daughters as a way of apology for her mood swings. At the time, Fareeda felt anger towards her mother, for the sadness she carried and brought into their home. She would distance herself, imagine her family was across the road with Rooqia where there was laughter, the busyness of family and a sense of belonging. A homeliness Rooqia had managed to keep a hold of in her own life: three children, a husband, a tidy semi-detached home in Fishponds.

'I think I've met someone,' Rooqia had winked, as they sat in Fareeda's small new flat in East London. They dunked gulab jamun into pink tea, teaspoons clinking in excitement. Almond crumbs scattered against the wooden dining table that was wedged between the kitchen door and the fridge. Fareeda sat on the table, her feet placed neatly on the dining chair next to Rooqia. At the time, Fareeda and her husband were both starting their new careers, and all the love they had felt for one another while they dated seemed like a distant memory in the face of bills to pay and laundry to wash. Fareeda had not noticed the cracks in her marriage, how they would avoid spending time together, how every family event seemed like an overwhelming obligation, a tiring act. How each of them relished having the flat to themselves. How they spent less time with their couple friends, and more time with people who knew them as individuals. It was slow and gradual, and when the reality of separation hit, they were the only two people shocked that the relationship had fallen apart. Rooqia was prepared and ready when a sobbing Fareeda had turned up at her door in the middle of the night, still in her robe and slippers. Humza quietly gave the two women their privacy, and allowed Fareeda the time she needed with her friend. Humza was similar to Rooqia in many ways. And he made Rooqia feel safe. Whenever Fareeda spent time with Rooqia and her new family, she would be reminded of her mother. A sudden pang would slowly fall into the pit of her stomach. On leaving her friend's house she would repeat duas, in fear that her hurt might cause a nazar on this happy little home.

Weeks later, when Rooqia messaged her to come cycling, Fareeda was reluctant. Her home was still in boxes, she had no plan; she knew she would not unpack, but instead sit in her pyjamas, her TV on, with rounds of tea and toast for company. Her days consisted of lying in bed for hours, staring at the ceiling, her stomach rumbling and her breath caught. She hated to look at the clock. Instead, she would listen to her neighbours upstairs, hear them as they woke, plodding around the kitchen, walking back and forth to the bathroom, the squeaking of their bed. In the evenings she would listen to the faint noise from their TV, their laughter, the clatter of pots and pans in the kitchen. She imagined that was her life instead.

Imagined herself walking around a tastefully decorated room, dancing while making dinner and calling out to someone in another room, to join her for dinner. In this alternate life she would complain how boring it all was, how wasted she was in her career, all the while relishing the security of it.

She wishes she could call her mother. Tell her *I am sorry*. But time has its own plan. When she had the chance, she wasted it. Now there is only the ghost of her mother and the FaceTime calls with her sister left to realise what her blessings were after all this time. She thinks of her sister in Australia — home meant very little to her, and Fareeda envies her nomadic resilience.

Fareeda watches the greengrocer across the road as he restocks heart-red pomegranates into the display boxes. He gives the coriander a gentle shake, and walks back into the shop. A few cars drive by. Two women with children in prams, deep in conversation, walk towards the alley between the café and the mosque. Their ponytails swing in unison, sunglasses reflecting back the sky.

'There is no shame in starting from scratch,' Rooqia had reassured her upon her return to Bristol. 'You need the drawing board sometimes. Hometowns are supposed to give you a sense of belonging, a place to rest and gather your thoughts. Then you begin again. At least you can say you tried. Nothing is braver than that.'

Rooqia had smiled her big smile, the gap showing between her two front teeth. Her face was framed by her black hijab, the pins glinting in the light. Fareeda often wondered how their friendship had survived all these years. Rooqia, who thought everything through, precise and sensible; and then Fareeda, tumbling through life, jumping two feet in, drowning in her poor decision making.

Some days, Fareeda would experience a spurt of energy and force herself to get used to her new life. Once, she headed out to her local gardening store and browsed for sturdy, low maintenance plants – heathers and lavender, aloe vera for her bedroom. As soon as she got home, she re-potted the plants in her communal garden, ready to place them on her windowsills. When she opened the garden shed, to her shock, she saw her Boardman. It had been carefully placed next to some broken garden chairs. It took her a while to recognise it. At first, she thought the cycle belonged to her neighbours upstairs. Then, as she got closer, the green shone at her and stopped her in her tracks. She had not expected to see the cycle again since her divorce – when her ex-husband had turned up and placed last year's fortieth birthday gift quietly in the shed, she did not know.

Seeing the cycle there made all the feelings Fareeda had suppressed come flooding back. To her surprise, she felt tears brimming in the corners of her eyes; she closed them tight, willed herself to move beyond the emotion. When she opened her eyes, she looked around hesitantly as though expecting to find her ex-husband there in the garden with her. But the garden was still and bright. The wooden decking under her bare feet was dirty and in need of a good clean. She sat down and held her knees. Took a deep breath. She would sell the cycle.

Fareeda walked back to the shed. The cycle sat there a mute, painful memory. Carefully, she brought the cycle into her home, ready to photograph and upload to a marketplace app. Another thing to add to her to-do list.

Over the course of the next few weeks, she had watched her garden closely. Stared at it while making cups of tea. Sat near her window while filling in applications for new jobs. Ever since she found out her ex-husband had visited she could not help but think about the past, as though it was something she could still capture. That time and distance could fix the hurt of an empty garden. Stood alone in such a communal space with only her shadow stretched out before her, surrounded by neglected plant pots, Fareeda felt how much life was slipping away. But there was another version of her life in that garden. The realisation did not scare her, but instead made the world around her expand. She suddenly felt ridiculous in her melodrama – there was more to life than her stacked boxes and empty garden.

'Hey!'

Rooqia is panting as she places her cycle next to Fareeda's. She pulls out a chair opposite and plonks herself down.

'Urgh, I'm tired already!'

'Let me remind you this was your idea,' Fareeda half jokes with her. 'No one is forcing you.'

Rooqia helps herself to Fareeda's chai, breaks into her dessert. She is dressed in serious cycling kit: gloves, reflective wear, black hijab wrapped low at the back of her hair, her helmet neatly placed on top. Fareeda feels silly in her jeans and hoodie. She has spent the last few days watching hundreds of YouTube tutorials, mobile phone connected to the front of her cycle while trying to get her balance in the courtyard garden. She had held the bars tightly and felt a huge flutter in her chest, her legs wobbly as she worried about her knuckles and the gravel below.

'Take your other foot off the ground. Take it off. Trust yourself.' Rooqia, like a parent, holding on to the back of her bike, ready to let her go.

Now, they stand on the pavement, ready for her first real ride. Rooqia sees her nervousness and, after wolfing down Fareeda's chocolate samosa, smiles her gap-toothed smile.

'You ready?'

'I guess.'

Rooqia laughs and puts her arm around Fareeda's shoulders, gives her a tight squeeze.

'There's a whole city waiting for you. You are here, so

make the most of it. Besides, I've seen you fall flat on your face worse than anything a cycle can do. Plus we'll be back by 7pm. I've got dinner ready for us.'

Rooqia, never one to allow anyone to wallow in self-pity.

Fareeda looks at the green cycle leaning against the cycle post. It shines in the sun. She takes a deep breath, senses the mosque – gold-patterned and full of prayers behind her – and mounts her cycle.

Today she lays to rest all the ghosts.

Bismillah. We cannot be everything at once.

About the Contributors

Helen Dunmore was an award-winning novelist, children's author and poet, renowned for the fluidity and lyricism of her prose, and her extraordinary ability to capture the past. She was the author of more than 50 books – novels, short story collections, poetry, and children's books. Her best known works include *Zennor in Darkness*, *A Spell of Winter* and *The Siege*, and her last book of poetry *Inside the Wave*. She won the inaugural Orange Prize for Fiction, the National Poetry Competition, and posthumously the Costa Book Award.

K.M. Elkes is the author of the short fiction collection *All That Is Between U*s (Ad Hoc Fiction, 2019). Individual short stories have won or been placed at the Manchester Fiction Prize, Royal Society of Literature Prize, and Bridport Prize. He was longlisted for the BBC National Short Story Award in 2019. He is from a rural, working class background, and his work reflects marginalised voices and places. He is currently writing a debut novel.

Christopher Fielden is an award-winning and Amazon bestselling author, and an award-winning editor. His work has been featured in books published by independent press, established magazines and renowned competition anthologies. In 2019, Victorina Press published Chris's short story collection, *Book of the Bloodless Volume 1: Alternative Afterlives*. The book was an Award-Winning Finalist in the 'Fiction: Short Story' category of the International Book Awards. You can learn

more about Chris on his website: www.christopherfielden.
com

Tessa Hadley is the author of six highly acclaimed novels and three short-story collections. In 2016 she was awarded the Windham Campbell Prize and the Hawthornden Prize. She teaches literature and creative writing at Bath Spa University. Her stories appear regularly in *The New Yorker, Granta* and other magazines.

Co-founder of Kiota Bristol and the Yoniverse Collective, **Shagufta K Iqbal** is an award-winning writer, workshop facilitator and TedX Speaker. She has been described by gal-dem as a poet whose work 'leaves you validated but aching – her narratives are important, heart-wrenching and relatable.' Her poetry collection *Jam Is For Girls, Girls Get Jam* has been recommended by Nikesh Shukla as 'a social political masterclass.' Her short poetry film 'Borders' has won several awards and been screened internationally. Shagufta is currently writing her second poetry collection and a debut novel.

Jamaican born **Valda Jackson** is an award-winning visual artist and writer. She was shortlisted for the prestigious National Windrush Monument commission in 2021, and designed the Royal Mint coin (due May 2023) to commemorate the 75th anniversary of Windrush. The untitled manuscript of Jackson's first novel was shortlisted for the Bath Spa Prize, 2021 by Janklow & Nesbit; and she is a recipient of the coveted Hawthornden Fellowship (2023). Jackson's short stories appear in anthologies including *The Peepal Tree Book of Caribbean Short Stories* (2018) *Closure: Contemporary Black British Short Stories* (Peepal Tree Press 2015), and online MMXX, (Bath Spa University (2022).

Asmaa Jama is a Danish-born Somali poet and 'multidisciplinary artist interested in ancestors, ghosts and diaspora lines. As a writer, they have been published in print and online in *The Poetry Review, The Good Journal, Ambit*, and *Popshot Magazine*, and have been commissioned by places such as Hayward Gallery, Arnolfini and Jerwood Arts.. And have been commissioned by places like Hayward Gallery, Arnolfini and Jerwood Arts. Their poetry has been shortlisted for the Wasafiri Writing Prize, The Brunel African Poetry Prize and the James Berry Poetry Prize and longlisted for the National Poetry competition. In 2020, Asmaa was a BBC New Creative, and in collaboration with Gouled Ahmed, created *Before We Disappear*, an interactive experience looking at hypervisibility/invisibiltiy. This year, they were commissioned by Bristol Old Vic to create *The Season of Burning Things*.

Sanjida Kay has had four psychological thrillers published by Corvus Books: *Bone by Bone, The Stolen Child, My Mother's Secret* and *One Year Later. Bone by Bone* went straight into the Amazon kindle best-selling list. It was long listed for the CWA Steel Dagger Award and nominated as one of the best crime and thriller books of 2016 by the Guardian and the Sunday Express. Her short story, 'The Beautiful Game', was published in *The Perfect Crime* (Harper Collins).

Heather Marks (co-editor) is a producer, editor, and writer. She is a longtime member of Words of Colour, where she creates meaningful opportunities for writers of colour, and from 2019 to 2022, she was part of the 'tiny but mighty' indie press No Bindings. She is currently working on a debut novel of historical fiction for young adults.

Joe Melia (co-editor) is the co-ordinator of the Bristol Short Story Prize, a bookseller, editor, and creative writing teacher. He has also been Bristol 24/7's Books and Spoken Word editor, a library assistant, and had numerous book reviews published.

Magnus Mills is the author of *A Cruel Bird Came to the Nest* and *Looked In* and six other novels, including *The Restraint of Beasts*, which won the McKitterick Prize and was shortlisted for both the Booker Prize and the Whitbread (now the Costa) First Novel Award in 1999. His novel *The Field of the Cloth of Gold*, was published to great critical acclaim and shortlisted for the Goldsmiths Prize 2016. His most recent novel, *The Forensic Records Society*, was published by Bloomsbury in April 2017. His books have been translated into twenty languages.

Rebecca Watts grew up in Avonmouth and Shirehampton in Bristol. She now lives in Brighton where she develops social work practice for children living in foster care. She also teaches social work at the University of Sussex and has written for academic publication. 'Going Down Brean' was shortlisted for the first Bristol Short Story Prize in 2008.

Special Thanks

The editors would like to thank the authors for their enthusiasm for this project, as well as Helen Dunmore's family, plus Ra Page, Kirstie Millar and Zoe Turner at Comma Press, Becky Percival at United Artists, Charlotte Osment at PRH, Olivia Kumar at RCW, and Kat Aitken. The publisher would like to thank Millie and Sally Shenton.

READING THE CITY (IN TRANSLATION)